PAGANS

Also in Scholastic Press:

Madame Retsmah Predicts
Michael Coleman

Brother, Brother, Sister, Sister
Zillah and Me
Helen Dunmore

Batty the Hero
The Hummingbird Secret
Susan Gates

The Dragon Upstairs
My Second-Best Friend
Geraldine Kaye

Ice Cat
Linda Newbery

Firehead
K.M. Peyton

Harry and the Wrinklies
Ragboy, Rats and the Surging Sea
The Brave Whale
Alan Temperley

The Girl in the Blue Tunic
Whistle and I'll Come
Jean Ure

PAGANS

SUSAN GATES

SCHOLASTIC
PRESS

Scholastic Children's Books,
Commonwealth House, 1–19 New Oxford Street,
London WC1A 1NU, UK
a division of Scholastic Ltd
London ~ New York ~ Toronto ~ Sydney ~ Auckland
Mexico City ~ New Delhi ~ Hong Kong

First published in the UK by Scholastic Ltd, 2000

Copyright © Susan Gates, 2000

Cover illustration by Mark Preston

ISBN 0 439 01469 7

Typeset by DP Photosetting, Aylesbury, Bucks.
Printed by Cox & Wyman Ltd, Reading, Berks.
10 9 8 7 6 5 4 3 2 1

CHAPTER ONE

Alice knew she couldn't hide in the glasshouse for ever. Soon they would come looking for her. "Go outside, Miss," they'd order her. "Get some fresh air."

Cook had just driven her out of the linen room, where it was warm and smelled of fresh laundry. It was even warmer in here. But it made her homesick. The air smelled so hot and flowery. And they grew the same tall, red lilies that grew like weeds at home after the rains.

Alice hated this English cold. And they told her it was Spring! She hated English clothes too. Especially gloves and heavy, thick coats and stockings and corsets.

Aunt Evaline thought it frightful that Alice had never worn corsets. "You poor girl, we must get you corseted. But none of those old fashioned lace-up-the-back things. This is 1907. The modern girl must have modern corsets."

Alice scratched over her shoulder. The hard corset rubbed at her back. It made those old burn scars scaly and sore.

At least the corset fastened at the front – so Alice didn't need a maid to help her dress. She didn't want anyone to see her back, with its dreadful knotted scars.

"Ah, there you are, Miss Silent-And-Say-Nothing –"

Cook came puffing in, in her snowy-white uniform. Alice hated her too. "She reminds me of Death," thought Alice, "in those white grave clothes. She's a big fat white Mama."

Alice was white too. Strangely, she'd hardly remembered that fact back in Africa. But here she remembered it all the time.

She thought of Ma and Pa, who were poor missionaries, teaching African children under mango trees. That had been her school too. But now she'd been sent back to England on a steamboat, to live with Aunt Evaline in Pagan Hill House. And attend a school for young ladies.

"I don't know, I'm sure," fussed Cook, as she shooed Alice like a chicken out of the glasshouse door. "Do I have to keep my eye on you every blessed second? Always skulking around in corners –"

In her mind, Alice called Cook a terrible name in Zulu. She cursed her, and her family, and hoped that the udders of all her cows would wither up and drop off.

"It's high time you went outside," said Cook. "Got some nice healthy red in them yellow cheeks. You shouldn't be such a trial. Not when your aunt is so poorly."

"You wouldn't boss me about," thought Alice, "if you knew I'd stroked a chameleon."

But Cook didn't know about chameleons. She didn't know they were witches in disguise and if you touched their skin you died – except that Alice had touched one and lived.

"I've got more power than you, big fat white Mama," thought Alice. "You ought to be afraid of me. I could change you into a fly."

But she said nothing. Since she'd arrived in England, three weeks ago, she'd been silent most of the time. Just watching – and learning how to survive. There were traps everywhere. Not only corsets but flush toilets – and button boots. In Africa, she went barefoot, like the other children.

Aunt Evaline didn't understand. She thought white people in Africa lived in fine style – in big, shady bungalows on hills. And belonged to the Officers' Club and went to each other's parties. But Alice and her family didn't live like that. Their home was a mud hut with sacking for a door curtain. They never, ever got asked to white people's parties.

Besides, even if they *had* been invited, just getting to their nearest white neighbour took a week's bone-shaking ride in an ox wagon.

"Want to be my sweetheart?" a stable lad had teased Alice, on her first day at Pagan Hill House. "What, cat got your tongue?"

Alice had been Miss Silent-And-Say-Nothing. But, inside her head, she'd had plenty to say – including the curse about crocodiles lying in wait at his waterhole.

"Come here, Miss," said Cook. "Young English ladies should have tidy hair. Not all bristly, like them fuzzy-wuzzies you was born amongst in Africa."

Alice thought of her African friends, with their oiled and tightly plaited hair. So sleek their heads looked like seals'. But she said nothing.

And when Cook tugged her hair into place, she said, "Thank you, thank you." Alice had learned that in England you must say, "Thank you, thank you," every minute. You must apologize, "Oh pardon. Sorry," even if people trod on *your* toes!

Alice dodged under Cook's arm. Across the cobbled scullery yard and into Pagan Hill House. She was in the kitchen passage now. It smelled of fresh-sliced cucumbers – Cook was making sandwiches for afternoon tea.

That was another thing about Pagan Hill House that filled Alice with wonder. The food. Every day here was a feast day! So much meat – great roasted hunks of it. Big plump hens, not scrawny ones like at home. And those puddings. Wobbly castles of creamy blancmange, sugar-frosted grapes so sweet they set your teeth tingling.

At every meal Alice imagined the amazed cries of her African friends, "*Eeeee*. Is all this food for us?" if she could magically fly them here and sit them down round Aunt Evaline's table.

She was just about to slip into the linen room, her other favourite hiding place, when she heard shouts from inside. Alice recognized the voice. It was Bertha, the head housemaid. An ancient woman with a face as whiskery as an old monkey.

"I've caught you," cried Bertha's voice. "Hiding in here again."

"I'm cold," complained a snivelling voice. "My bones ache – it's so lovely and warm in here."

"That sounds like me," thought Alice, in a few seconds of dizzy confusion. But how could that be? She couldn't be in two places at once, in there and out here, listening, at the door. She wasn't a witch doctor.

"Then who is it?" thought Alice. "Who is it in there? Who gets aching bones from the cold, and hides in the linen room to get warm – just like me?"

In England she hadn't met anyone remotely like herself. Ever since she'd arrived she'd felt like a freak, a complete outsider. She kept breaking the rules. She didn't mean to, but there were so many of them. Some they didn't even *tell* you about. They kept them secret. Then laughed when you made a stupid mistake –

Gloves, for instance. There were masses of rules about them. Young ladies must not shake hands without gloves. You were allowed to take them off when visiting. But only to eat cake. And then only if it was messy like chocolate cake. If it was dry, crumbly cake, you kept your gloves on. It make her head spin, just remembering all the rules about gloves. But how was she supposed to know? She'd never, in the whole of her life, even worn a pair of gloves!

Inside the linen room, Bertha was shouting again.

"You shouldn't be here!" she was shrieking at someone. "You should be out there, polishing the jelly moulds. And by the way, there's one missing –"

"I told you, the pagans borrowed it," shivered the other voice. "The same as that kettle that disappeared. They borrowed that too."

"Pagans? Pagans? Don't you talk to me about pagans!" screamed Bertha in a frenzy. "You need your head examining, my girl—"

Alice moved away from the door. She shook herself like a half-drowned lion cub. These three weeks in England had seemed like a dream. Lots of wondrous things had happened. She'd been out in the carriage with Aunt and Aunt had said. "Look! There's a cro-codile!" And Alice had looked. "Where? Where?" pleased at last to recognize something. But all she'd seen was a long line of schoolgirls walking along two by two. "That is one of our *English* crocodiles," Aunt Evaline had insisted. So Alice was used to English strangeness. But the conversation she'd just overheard inside the linen room – that seemed like the strangest thing of all.

Who were the pagans? Did they live *here*, at Pagan Hill House? Why did they borrow jelly moulds? Were they especially fond of jelly? She shrugged and gave up. Just one more thing she didn't understand.

Alice climbed the stone steps, went through the green baize doors. She was in the front of the house now, where all the stairs had carpets. The back of the house, Alice had learned, was for servants, with Cook as their Chief. The front of the house belonged to the family. It was very grand. And so quiet. At the moment, it was quiet as the grave.

Then a feeble, sickly wail came from somewhere upstairs.

"It's still alive then," thought Alice. She was surprised. In their village, babies who cried like that would not have lived long.

Three days ago, Aunt Evaline had given birth, early, to a baby boy. Both their lives had been in danger. The doctor's motorcar was outside the house day and night. Servants rushed up and down, fetching and carrying. No one had time for the wary, wild child from Africa. Who hardly dared open her mouth, except to say, "Sorry" or "Thank you". Who was as twitchy as a gazelle. Whose belly was burning because she was not used to rich food and whose heart ached because she longed so much to go home.

"We shouldn't have kept you with us so long," Ma had said, as if they'd been very selfish parents. "You're already fourteen. And your uncle is well-off. He says he will pay for your schooling. What a lucky girl to have such kind, generous relatives."

Alice had never seen her uncle. He was a soldier far away in India – a colonel in the Guards. He didn't even know yet that his son had been born. "Such a fine man, your uncle," said Cook. "Such handsome black whiskers!"

Back safe in her bedroom, Alice gazed out at the damp English parkland and tried hard to be grateful. She had been given wonderful presents; things she had never dreamed of. A parasol (with frills), a silver-backed hairbrush, a white chiffon dress – gifts her friends at home would go pop-eyed to see. She knew she was very lucky. She was trying hard to fit in. But every time she thought about Africa it sent a sharp pain to her heart.

"Aunt Evaline is awfully nice!" she told herself. "*Awfully*," and was proud of using the latest slang, a word she'd heard the housemaids use. She was worried about Aunt Evaline and the baby. She said a quick prayer that they would live.

Her bedroom window was open a crack. She went to close it to keep out the chill. Why did nobody here mind the cold as much as she did? Except that voice in the linen room. Whoever that belonged to hated cold too.

And then she heard the voice again. She was sure it was the same one. It was wailing, just as it had before. Only this time, it wasn't inside the house. It seemed to be out there, in the parkland.

Alice pushed up her window and leaned out, with her hands gripping the sill. It was grey and a little misty outside. She could see, through the white haze, a sea of blue flowers under the trees. Bluebells, those flowers were called. Aunt Evaline had told her that.

"You must have been hearing things," Alice decided. From behind her, from somewhere down long corridors, came the wail of the sick baby. "It must have been that you heard," she told herself.

Then she heard the voice again. It came drifting creepily through the mist. It was outside, she was sure of it. And, at the same time, she saw a light – a flash of brilliant light through the trees. Like the sudden glare of a leopard's eyes, deep in the bush.

She waited, her heart fluttering.

Then the voice came again. Only this time Alice could hear what it said. "Let me in," it moaned, pathetically. "Why won't you let me in?"

CHAPTER TWO

That voice could have been Alice's own. Its bewildered cry matched her mood exactly. She had to find out who it belonged to. It sounded to Alice like someone as mixed-up as she was. Someone who took their gloves off when they shook hands. And kept them on while eating chocolate cake.

That reminded her. She paused for a moment to tug on those dratted gloves. A young lady mustn't go out without them – that was a strict rule. As far as Alice knew it might be the *law*. Perhaps policemen came up and questioned you, if you forgot to wear them.

She slipped down the stairs. As she passed the ballroom she just had to glance inside. After three weeks, it still made her sigh with wonder. It sparkled with tall mirrors and long windows. Aunt Evaline had said, "Of course, my dear, we are hardly *rich*. This is nowhere as grand as *most* people's ballrooms." When Alice had told her, in an awed whisper: "But I've never seen anything so splendid, in my entire life," Aunt Evaline had smiled and patted her niece's hair and said, "Poor little innocent. How simply sweet!"

Alice glimpsed herself, just for a second, reflected in one of the glittering mirrors. She hardly recognized herself. Pale and anxious in a white, gauzy dress, she looked like a ghost child. It gave her a bad fright. She seemed to be fading away almost as she watched. She fled, out of Pagan Hill House, past the doctor's motorcar and into the mist.

There were no more flashing lights. No more cries – only woodpigeons softly cooing. She stood absolutely still, looking around, listening. She was pretty sure the cries had come from the woodland, by the ornamental lake.

She suddenly remembered her aunt's warnings: "Don't wander alone in the woodland, dear. It's a wild place. Keep to the *civilized* bit of the garden – the lawns and the gravel paths."

"A wild place?" thought Alice, with a wondering frown. The worst she could do here was make her shoes wet, tear her dress on the thorns. Were there leopards here? No. Not even scorpions or snakes. This wasn't like the African bush, where you never wandered alone.

She thought of the time she and her friend Mayamiko had been stalked through the bush by – *something*. It had moved in closer, closer, in complete silence. They never saw it. All they saw were two golden eyes. Only baboons, whooping and crashing through trees, scared it off.

"Was that a leopard?" asked Alice, when it was gone.

Mayamiko had shrugged. "Perhaps. Or perhaps it was an evil spirit."

Or the time Ma had nearly stepped on a boomslang snake. One bite from that and you died. And her friend Neema had killed the snake with a stick. Crushed its spine. Then she'd opened it up and found six tiny chicks in its belly. It had been sliding along branches and robbing nests of their babies.

Alice looked up into the oak trees. She grinned at herself for thinking a boomslang might drop down and coil round her neck. "You are in England now," she told herself. "No need to worry about danger. These woods are safe."

Why was she shivering though? Then, with a jolt of panic, she realized: "You've forgotten your coat. And that sailor-hat Auntie bought you. You are not properly dressed."

What if a policeman saw her?

Alice was just about to make a mad dash back to the house, when she heard someone weeping. They were sobbing their heart out.

She stepped out of the trees, on to the path that led round the lake. And, at once, forgot all about hats and coats. Because there, by the side of the path, was a grassy mound. It burst out of the ground like a giant green pimple. On top of this hill, hugging it, like a starfish hugs a rock, was a girl. She was bundled up in a blue canvas apron – the kind maids wear for cleaning out grates. Her hair was a frizzy mess.

Alice saw all this in one astonished stare. Then she saw that the hill had a door in it. A wooden door, scarcely big enough for a child to crawl through. It was locked with a rusty padlock and crusty with lichens. It looked as if it hadn't been opened for years.

Alice stood there, chewing the ends of her gloves, tormented by doubt. What would be the correct behaviour? It was rude to stare, she'd learned that almost as soon as she'd stepped off the steamboat. Should she pass by, pretending she hadn't seen? How do you greet a girl who's weeping buckets and hugging a hill? There were probably rules about it.

In the end, she gave a discreet little cough, "*Hem, hem,*" behind her glove. She was pleased with how polite and English she sounded.

The girl on the hill turned a wild, tear-stained face towards her. "These rotten pagans," she said, in a surprisingly fierce, unladylike voice. "They won't let me in. Ain't it terrible? And I know they're listening. I told them. I said, 'See here, I can't stand this no more.' I told them, 'I'm losing heart, you know.' But they just don't care –"

There was no doubt about it. She was the girl warming her bones in the linen room – the one Bertha, the head housemaid, had been scolding.

And before Alice could stop herself, or think it was rude, she found herself blurting out questions. "Those pagans – are they the same ones that borrowed the jelly mould?"

The girl didn't seem at all put out: "The same," she said, raising her eyebrows and huffing a great, weary sigh. "They tease me something cruel. *And* get me into trouble. Sometimes I tell 'em, 'I'm going to have nothing more to do with you.' Last week they borrowed a kettle and Cook blamed me for it—"

A voice bellowed from the direction of the house. "Bessie, Bessie? Where are you, girl? Get back here this instant. Bessie?"

"That's me." Bessie startled Alice by springing off the mound like a grasshopper. "It's that Bertha, she makes my life a misery. She's hateful, she is," Bessie muttered, with a truly savage scowl. "She says I'm a clumsy girl. She says, 'You bang doors. You break plates. You butter-fingers.' "

This time, Alice kept quiet. She wasn't sure whether Bessie was really talking to her – or just grumbling away to herself.

Bessie looked too frail to be so ferocious. She was the most freakish child Alice had ever seen. Tiny and quick and birdlike with stick-like limbs and a strange withered-apple face that might have belonged to an old woman. It seemed like a puff of wind might blow her away – except for the big black boots she was wearing, and that heavy sack-like apron that wrapped round her twice and draggled in the mud.

"Don't matter though," snuffled Bessie, wiping the drips off her nose with her sleeve. "I'm more powerful than her. She ought to be scared of me. 'Cos one day, when I get my special powers, I'll change her into a beetle." And her wrinkled apple face lit up with glee at the thought.

Then she was off. Flitting like a blue bat through the trees. "She has special powers," thought Alice, amazed. "Like me." For one joyous, magical second she had a vision of Cook turned into a buzzing fly and Bertha into a beetle.

A cockroach would be better. At home they had some perfectly hideous cockroaches – bright orange ones, and giant, scuttling red ones with long, squirming feelers. You often found them swimming in the chamber pot under your bed.

Suddenly Alice had a desperate desire to tell Bessie about changing Bertha into an African cockroach. The kind that drowned in your po. She was certain that Bessie would think it a great joke. They would giggle about it together. Alice hadn't shared a joke with anyone since she landed on these shores.

She yelled after the tiny scurrying figure, "Come back! I have something funny to tell you –"

But Bessie had vanished.

For a moment Alice felt totally desolate. As if a possible friend had been snatched away from her.

And she was alone again amongst strangers who didn't understand.

She stared at the green hill, with its velvety grass. She walked around it. What was in there? Why did Bessie want to get in? It reminded her of the huge, dome-like ant hills on the African plains. But none of the ant hills she'd seen had little doors set in them.

Alice scratched her back thoughtfully – that corset was rubbing those old burn scars again. She tried to clear her head; think back to what Bessie had said: "They won't let me in. But I know they're listening."

So did pagans live in that hill then? Those cruel jelly mould borrowers who'd got Bessie into trouble? It made Alice's head ache, trying to untangle this bit of English strangeness.

"What do pagans look like?" she asked herself. Were they even *human*? It made her flesh creep, thinking of them inside the mound, listening. She gave a quick, scared glance at the padlocked door. If the pagans were in there, they couldn't get out. Unless they too, had magical powers—

"No," Alice told herself sternly. "This is an *English* wood! Such things *never* happen here!"

But she decided this wasn't a good place to linger.

"I'll go back and ask Cook," she reasoned with herself. "I'll ask her about pagans." She didn't like Cook. But at least she would get some straight answers.

The waters of the lake were changing from grey to black. Soon, it would be getting dark. At home, at this time, ghosts and spirits came out, one by one. When it was pitch dark the bush would be teeming with them – whooping and shrieking all night long. Now, at dusk, even these safe English woods had begun to feel creepy. And their chill cut right through to her bones.

"Serve you right," she scolded herself. "You are not properly dressed for outside, are you?" Shivering in her gauzy dress, she turned back towards the house.

Her nostrils twitched: "What's that smell?" It took her instantly back to Africa. It was a sweet, burnt-sugar smell, like young maize cobs roasted on a fire.

"Who's roasting maize?" she thought, astonished. "Here in England?"

Then she saw the light again – the one she had seen from her bedroom window. Bright white and eerie, it flashed through the trees. Just like a witch light –

Her friends had told her about witch lights. They'd told her many African stories. Stories Alice couldn't tell Pa because Pa disapproved of such things. "Ignorant superstition," he called them. But he was always away, travelling for days in the ox wagon, tending the sick and saving souls. And Ma was often too weak to move – the heat didn't agree with her. So Alice was left to wander barefoot and free.

She knew many tales Pa wouldn't approve of. The story about witch lights was one every child knew – when a witch wanted to trap you, she sent a magical ball of glittering light. You got into a terrible state. You thought, "Oh no. Is that a witch light? I must run away!" But that was a big mistake. For you'd run straight into the witch's scrawny arms. "Got you!" she'd cry out, licking her lips. An African child knew, if they saw a witch light, that they must stay calm. They must walk *directly* towards it – away from the wicked witch. Only then would they be safe.

"This is England," Alice reminded herself again, in her sternest, most sensible voice. "There are no spirits, no witch lights here to trap you. There's no dangerous magic like that."

But her heart was still back in Africa. And, despite what her head told her, it gave her more urgent orders: *That witch is waiting to catch you. Walk towards the light.*

Alice started walking, trance-like, through the gloomy wood. There was the light again, up in the tree branches. One brilliant flash, like a shooting star, then it was gone. That burnt sugar smell was even stronger. Witch lights and roasting maize? Alice stopped then, afraid and confused. What on earth was going on in this *English* wood?

In the next clearing was a low-spreading cedar tree. Some of its branches swept the ground. Alice took some uncertain steps towards it. Bramble thorns tugged at her woollen stockings. Horrified, she bent down to unhook them – young ladies must not spoil their stockings – when something rustled in the cedar tree above her head. An animal, a very *big* animal –

"Leopard," thought Alice, in a panic. Leopards sat up trees, in the heat of the day.

She sprang out of the way and crashed into the tree trunk. It tried to cling on to her; wouldn't let her go. It was sticky, like the web of a great spider. Her white gauzy dress was glued to the bark.

"Help!" cried Alice, her mind swirling with panic. She ripped herself free from the tree. She went sprawling to the ground and when she looked up, into the dark mass of branches, she saw two glittering eyes, peering at her out of the woody bark.

"This tree has eyes," Alice's brain gabbled at her. "It has a spirit inside it. It's an evil, child-catching tree –"

That sweet sugar smell lured children into its trap. And then they got stuck, poor things, like flies on flypaper. Aunt Evaline was right about this English wood. She shouldn't be wandering here alone. It had more dangerous magic than the bush – this tree was more cunning than witch lights. She must escape –

Her heart in a wild-beating frenzy, she got up to run. Too late. Crash! A tree-man came leaping down. He crouched frog-like in the grass. He had a tree-trunk head. For a bewildering second Alice was back in Africa – watching the witch doctor in his wooden mask spinning and stamping to the drums.

Then she saw that the tree-man was dressed in English country clothes – a Norfolk jacket, knicker-bockers and leggings.

A voice came out of the tree-trunk head. A very English voice. "I say," it exclaimed. "Did I give you a rotten scare? I'm fearfully sorry and all that."

CHAPTER THREE

Alice felt stupid. She had felt like that from the moment the boy pulled off his tree-trunk mask and told her, "I was only doing some photography..."

How could she have thought that this ordinary tree had a spirit inside it? That it was out to catch children? Every word the boy said made her fears seem more foolish.

"See here," said the boy, holding up the hollowed-out piece of tree trunk. "I made it myself – I read about it in a book on wildlife photography. It has two eye-holes – so I can see out. And birds come right up to me and think I'm part of the tree. Then I can easily take their pictures. It's a frightfully useful piece of kit."

Alice felt tongue-tied and wary. She knew photography was a new craze – Aunt Evaline had a Kodak she hadn't learned how to use yet. So not knowing about photography was not too embarrassing. But not knowing about English boys was. She wasn't used to speaking with English boys. There must be strict rules – even stricter than about gloves. But she hadn't a clue what they were.

This boy didn't seem to care too much about rules. He was as friendly as a puppy. He'd shown her his camera – a wooden box with dangling legs, like a giant dead spider.

"It's the very latest thing!" he'd told her. "It's got a Dallmeyer lens and Thornton and Pickard's silent shutters."

And Alice had nodded politely as if she understood. She wanted to seem cool and serene, like Aunt Evaline. But she felt as jumpy as a deer at a waterhole.

"I smelled sugar and thought—" she began. Then stopped herself just in time. Best not to mention what she'd thought – that the tree was an evil spirit. He'd only think she needed her head examining.

"I sugared the tree," the boy said, as if any fool should know that. "It's what we photographers do. To attract moths, you know, so we can snap them. Want to know how to do sugaring? It's simple. Just get treacle, and water, and one pound of brown sugar and boil it all up. It's a glorious mess, it smells like toffee. And then you paint it on the tree and, hey presto, the moths come. I say, I'm awfully sorry, did it spoil your dress?"

"I – I saw lights," said Alice. And again, she stopped short. She mustn't say she believed they were witch lights. Those were *African* thoughts. She must try from now on to be sensible − like a well-brought-up English young lady.

"Ahh," said the boy, with a grin keen as mustard. "Lights like this?" he crouched down, found something in a big canvas bag, then stood up again.

A flash of white fire split the gloom. It was dazzling; it hurt her eyes. Alice shied away like a spooked pony. She hated fire − it always meant pain and terror for her. Ever since, when she was a toddling baby, she had fallen backwards on to a cooking fire in an African hut. Ma had snatched her out. But it was too late, the glowing wood had burned her back. The skin was white and shiny and puckered − there were thick burn scars like twisted ropes.

Alice had hidden her back from Aunt Evaline and the maids. She didn't want anyone to see it. At home, there were other village children who'd fallen in cooking fires. Some were burnt far worse than she was. But English girls were supposed to have clear pink skin. Blushing, rose-petal skin − she'd seen pictures in Aunt Evaline's fashion magazines. People here thought her face was yellowy, sickly-looking. What would they think if they saw her back? What would this boy think?

Alice hugged herself tightly to stop herself shuddering. "The fire's gone. It's all right. It's all right," she was babbling, over and over again, inside her head.

"It was only my magnesium ribbon," explained the boy in alarm. "I was just showing you. You light it and, flash, you can get photos in bad light, even at night. Pretty good, isn't it?"

Alice dragged some cold, damp air into her shaking body. She felt a bit better now, not so dizzy and faint.

"Oh no, I feel like a worm," said the boy, in an anguished voice. "I've scared you to death again. Honour bright, I didn't mean it. You look white as a ghost." Then he added, in a voice more curious than guilt-ridden. "I say, are you the girl who's come all the way from Africa?"

"Yes," Alice nodded, nervously. She felt unreal, part of a fantastical dream. She had just met a freakish child on a mound who said the pagans wouldn't let her in. And now this boy. He wore wooden masks. He hid up trees, smeared them with sugar and scared her with fires. Who was he? Where did he come from? She wondered if she should shake hands. Did you keep your gloves on or take them off when you did that? Her brain was too scrambled; she couldn't remember.

"I've only been here for three weeks," she said. She almost blurted out, "And this is a *most peculiar* country." But she decided that wasn't polite. And besides, no one would believe her. They thought *here* was normal. They thought corsets and wobbly puddings shaped like castles were normal. They thought *Africa* was strange!

"Ahh," said the boy, as if everything was clear to him now. "No wonder you were scared into fits. You must be a perfect dunce about photography. Not your fault –

I would be too if I came from darkest Africa. Bet you don't even know what a telephoto lens is, do you?"

He set his camera up on its spidery legs, rummaged about in his bag of gear and found a long lens: "Course, I can't use it now, it's getting too dark. But I'll just show you, shall I?" He paused for a second, absorbed in screwing the lens on to his camera. "It's for snapping things that are far away. The other day, I photographed a kestrel's nest and—"

He never got a chance to tell Alice about the kestrel. A bundle of fury came shrieking out of the trees and leapt upon the boy's back like a blue demon.

"Don't shoot them," it wailed, clawing at his face. "Don't shoot my poor pagans, Mister!"

The boy didn't hit out. He didn't panic. Instead he plucked Bessie's hands from his face with a calmness that left Alice gaping. Then he heaved her like a sack of feathers off his back and dumped her into the long grass.

"It's me, Richard," he said quickly, before she could maul him again. "Look at me, Bessie. I'm the doctor's son. You know me."

"Don't go firing that machine gun—"

"Hang it, Bessie, this isn't a machine gun, you ass. It's not to *kill* your precious pagans. It's for taking their picture. And, anyhow, I thought you were up at the house polishing jelly moulds—"

"I was," said Bessie in a rush, "but Cook said, 'I'm sick to death of things disappearing into thin air.' She sent me away. I told her, 'It's not my fault, I didn't take 'em, it's those pagans.' She said, 'If you weren't the gamekeeper's daughter and a favourite of the Mistress I'd have the police on you.' But Richard, could you really get a snap of my pagans with that camera thing? How could you see them anyhow? Humans can't see them. Even changelings like me can't see them. Not if the pagans don't want them to—"

"I'm sure *I* could get a picture," said Richard, defensively, as if she was challenging his photographic skills. "Well, *pretty* sure anyhow. There's a silent shutter on this camera. I could sneak up on 'em – they wouldn't hear me at all. And in my tree mask disguise, they wouldn't even know I was there."

Bessie's queer, old woman's face was suddenly brilliant with happiness. "I can't believe it," she said, breathlessly, clasping her tiny hands together. "I'm going to get a photograph of them. I'll treasure it my whole life. I will! I'd like it above anything! Oh thank you. Thank you."

"Look here, I only said I was *pretty* sure –" Richard warned her, alarmed by her frenzy of gratitude. But it was too late. She was gone, whisking away into the gloom between the trees.

Up at the Big House, a motorcar engine began to chunter. "That's my dad," said Richard, loading himself with all his gear, like a tinker with his pots and pans. "I'll have to go now. He gets fearful mad if he's kept waiting."

The doctor's son put his tweed cap on. And he was off too, staggering away through the wood.

When he was almost hidden by trees, he seemed to stop. "I say," he called back, "I forgot. There's something here should make you feel at home."

Alice pushed eagerly through branches to catch him up. "What is it?"

"A lion," he said.

Instantly Alice's heart was jerky with panic. "Where?" Her hand flew to her mouth. "Where?"

"There," said Richard, baffled by her terror. Her head whipped round. She saw two white bulging eyes, a milk-white curly mane –

"It's a *stone* lion," she said angrily. "A statue! And it doesn't look like a lion at all. I suppose it's an *English* lion?"

It was more Pekinese dog than lion. A square lion, with great bulging fish eyes, a mane of tight curls and a friendly grin. At once, the image vanished from her head – of that scraggy-maned, scrawny African lion, half-mad with hunger, that took Neema's little sister when she was out fetching water. And all they found was her gnawed leg bone –

"I think it might be, er, *Chinese* actually," Richard said, awkwardly. He swept his free hand around the wood. "There are some other statues round here, Greek ones and such. But I thought that this one, this one –" He stumbled into silence, tongue-tied at last by this strange African girl he wanted to welcome. But, somehow, kept scaring into fits.

A car horn honked urgently. He gave her one last helpless, embarrassed shrug. "Sorry," he said, "Sorry." Then staggered away again.

Alice sighed. She patted the stone lion's mossy head. He was a comical lion. Quite sweet really. "I think you are *definitely* an English lion," she told him. He was as harmless as English crocodiles.

She left him and wandered back to the sugar tree. She stood there for a long time. Her head should have been buzzing with questions. But it wasn't – instead she felt dazed, almost in a trance. The woods were dark and very quiet. The sugar smell mingled with the smell of scorched grass, where Richard had dropped the magnesium ribbon. At least it proved that he'd actually been there. But that Bessie might have been a dream.

The windows of Pagan Hill House were yellow oblongs, glowing through the trees. They seemed to spark Alice's brain into life again. She gave a little shiver, hugged herself in shaky arms, then trudged off towards the lights.

Cook was waiting for her. "Heaven help us, you look a perfect fright. We'd better tidy you up, my girl, before anybody sees you."

While Cook fussed and tutted and sponged at her dress Alice asked her, straight out, "Cook, what are pagans?"

Cook looked at her sharply. "That Bessie hasn't been filling your brain with her nonsense by any chance? She's simple-minded. Not right in the head." Cook tapped her own skull, significantly.

"She says she's a changeling," persisted Alice. "What does that mean?"

Cook gave a long-suffering sigh: "She thinks she's one of the fairy folk. Pagans is the old name for them round here. She thinks she was swapped at birth while her ma was busy doing the mangling."

"*Eeeeee!*" exclaimed Alice in amazement. Then remembered she was in England now. "Good gracious," she corrected herself.

Cook looked at her strangely. "You might well say 'good gracious'. This place might still be called Pagan Hill House. But no sensible person believes the old tales – about pagans living in hills hereabouts. Except that idiot girl Bessie, of course. And *she's* got it into her head that she's a pagan princess. I ask you!" Cook snorted in derision. "You don't want nothing to do with her," was Cook's grim warning. "She's a little thief. It beats me why your aunt is so soft with her. Now, if it was up to me –"

Cook ranted on about how she'd like Bessie locked up. Alice winced as Cook's hard hands dragged her hair back and screwed it into a tight bun. She didn't make a sound. But she thought, "You ignorant woman. One day Bessie will change Bertha into a beetle. And she'll probably change you too."

Her solemn, yellow face almost smiled when she thought of Bertha and Cook, two long, red cock-roaches, on their backs, their legs waving... What a delicious crunching sound it would make when you stepped on them with your boot.

"There," said Cook triumphantly. "Now you are fit to see your aunt."

"Can I?" All thoughts of beetles and Bessie and pagans fled from Alice's head. "Is Aunt Evaline well again? That baby – did it die?"

"*He* certainly did not!" said Cook, appalled. "How could you say such a thing, you cold-hearted child?"

"I have broken another rule," thought Alice, sadly, as Cook bustled before her up the stairs and through the green baize doors.

Seeing Aunt Evaline was a shock. She was Ma's little sister. But Alice had never seen much resemblance between them. Aunt Evaline was young and pretty – she had married a rich, handsome colonel, not a penniless missionary like Pa. She wore fashionable clothes and never had bristly hair. But today, she looked so much like Ma that Alice felt a black wave of homesickness rise up and almost drown her.

Aunt Evaline lay in a great, high bed. Her hair was spread out on the pillow. "It's untidy," Alice noted with surprise. "It's got tangles in. Why does no one brush them out?" Aunt Evaline's eyes were closed and her face looked as pale and worn-out as Ma's – on one of Ma's bad days.

Alice crept up to the bed. "Is she dead?" she almost asked Cook. But then she remembered it wasn't polite to speak of death, straight out like that. "Ma?" she whispered, without thinking, anxiously tugging at the quilted covers.

"Shhh!" hissed Cook, outraged. "Mistress is sleeping. She must have rest and quiet. And *you* must be a good child and keep out of the way. We can't be bothered with you just now."

Alice had learned very quickly that Cook resented her – as a poor relation, a charity case, a troublesome, freakish child who couldn't flush toilets. "Ugh, she makes my flesh creep," Alice had heard Cook tell Bertha. "It's the way she *watches* you all the time –" Alice had wanted to cry out: "I'm only watching because I don't know the rules!" But she had said nothing and sneaked away.

She said nothing now. But she didn't crumple at Cook's words. She had determined, in her own head, to be as proud and disdainful as a African princess. "I stroked a chameleon and lived," she told herself. "English cooks don't frighten me."

Suddenly Alice longed to see Bessie, that other freakish child, who thought herself a princess too. They had other things in common. Bessie liked warm places. She hated Cook. And she believed in magic.

"No one here wants me," Alice thought. "I'll go and find Bessie. And teach her some African curses."

33

Alice turned back to check on Aunt Evaline. She seemed to be sweetly sleeping. She had a warm bed, more food than she could eat and servants to wait on her. "She is bound to get well then," Alice reassured herself.

Then a thin, sickly wail came from the other side of the bed. From a rocking cradle all covered with frills.

"The new baby," thought Alice. "I had quite forgotten about it."

Nurse came hurrying in at the baby's cries.

"May I look at the baby?" Alice asked Nurse politely.

"Just a quick peek then," said Nurse, who was good-natured. "The poor little mite, he cries and cries. We can do nothing to quiet him."

Alice leaned over the cradle. She forgot staring was rude – and that speaking the honest truth was even ruder.

"Why," she said, amazed, "he is all shrivelled up like a baby baboon."

And she knew, from the way Cook frogmarched her out of the sick room, that she had broken another rule.

CHAPTER FOUR

When Alice woke up next morning she thought she was in Africa. She thought she saw geckos on her bedroom wall. At home, those tiny lizards whisked about everywhere. They were friends; they caught flies. And the most amazing thing was – some had transparent bodies. If they were up against the light you saw their tiny hearts beating. You could even see their neatly coiled-up insides.

Then, with a sigh, Alice saw that her eyes were playing tricks. They weren't geckos. They were just swirly patterns on her English wallpaper.

The bedroom felt icy cold when she slipped out from under her quilt. She could have been warm. She could have had a blazing fire set in the grate by a maid. But fires still gave her shuddering fits, even though it was years since she'd toppled, screaming, on to that glowing charcoal.

Her burns were itchy today.

"Dare I?" thought Alice.

She couldn't bear the thought of that stiff corset scraping those scars red raw. So she stuffed it down the back of her armchair.

"Please, please don't let anyone find it," she thought. But they probably would. There were always maids snooping around. Knocking on your door saying, "Miss, I've been sent up to do your room."

Alice knew this was serious rule-breaking. But to make up for it, she loaded on all the outdoor clothes she could find – hat, coat, gloves. Then wrapped a scarf round and round her neck until she was nearly strangled. She might be improperly dressed underneath. But on top she could pass Cook's most flinty-eyed inspection.

She found she wasn't much scared of Cook any more. All you had to do was think of her as a red, scuttling cockroach you could step on. *Crunch.* That seemed to work wonders.

She stuffed her breakfast toast into her coat pocket for later. She wanted to get away, before she was found out.

She passed Nurse on the stairs. Without Alice even having to ask, Nurse said: "Your aunt is much more herself this morning."

"Perhaps," thought Alice, "that means she has on her silks and jewels And isn't white and ill-looking like Ma any more." Thoughts of Ma were bad – they meant homesickness. So Alice shut Ma out of her mind.

"*Waaaa!*" That new baby was still wailing. "Will it never stop?" thought Alice. She wished she hadn't said last night that it looked like a baby baboon. She felt quite sorry for it now – twisting and crying and complaining. It didn't seem to like England much either.

"That's right. Get some fresh air. Put some roses in them yellow cheeks," said Cook, as Alice trundled through the kitchen in her heavy outdoor clothes.

"Cockroach," thought Alice, smiling politely.

"I see you look more cheery today," said Cook. "About time too. And you with everything to be thankful for."

"*Crunch*," thought Alice, smiling even more brightly, while secretly screwing the toe of her black boot into the flagstones.

She deliberately didn't go into the glasshouse. She didn't want to sniff that hot, flowery air, see those red lilies and start dreaming of home. She was trying to toughen herself up.

"You are stuck here," she told herself. "Until you finish school. So you had better make the best of it."

That was Ma's motto: "Make the best of what you have." And Pa would approve of his daughter being so strong-minded. He hated mopers.

"Oh no," thought Alice. "I'm thinking of Ma and Pa again." She had determined not to do that...

"I'm making the best of it, Ma," Alice assured Ma out loud as if Ma was there to hear her. "There's this girl, Bessie – I'm going to find her now. I think she may be my friend. *Eeeee*, she is a strange girl," Alice stopped speaking, awkwardly. She suddenly thought that Ma might not approve of Bessie, any more than Cook did. Pa certainly wouldn't. He would be truly shocked at an English child who thought she belonged to pagans and not to Jesus. He would have to save that child immediately.

Alice hastily ended her little talk to Ma with: "Well, I am fine and Aunt Evaline is fine and the new baby he cries all the time. But he is fine too. So don't worry, Ma. We are all perfectly fine here in England."

She was relieved to find that talking to Ma hadn't made her as homesick as all that.

She was round at the grand front entrance of Pagan Hill House now. There was the doctor's car, here already, parked on the gravel drive.

"I wonder if Richard has come with him," thought Alice.

She hadn't forgotten about the doctor's son. She'd been thinking about him a lot last night. But with much more caution than she thought about Bessie. She had no problem with Bessie's pagans. She knew Cook scorned them. But in Africa there were many things humans couldn't explain – hordes of strange, magical beings out there, in the dark. And they were always meddling in human lives. So it wouldn't surprise her at all if these pagans existed. What would *really* surprise her was a boy like Richard ending up as her sweetheart. Alice had already decided that having a sweetheart was a dream for a girl like her. Here in England even her *face* was wrong – all yellowy from a hot climate. Not anything like those rosy, blushing girls in Aunt Evaline's magazines.

Still, perhaps she and Richard might be friends – but she was even doubtful about that. She wasn't sure whether English rules allowed friendships with boys. Was it ladylike? Was it proper? It made her head ache just thinking about it.

She tried to stop thinking about Richard – it was too confusing. But she had crossed the lawns and was into the wild woodland now. She came across the stone lion with his doggy face and goldfish eyes.

"You're the silliest lion I ever saw," she told him and patted his neck as she passed. Then she found herself under Richard's tree – where he'd leapt down in his tree mask and scared her. She sniffed the bark. It still smelt very faintly of sugar. She couldn't help looking out for him.

"I wonder," she thought, "if he's taken that photo of pagans yet – the one he promised Bessie?" She hoped so. "Bessie would like that picture more than anything."

And Alice would like to see it herself. She wanted to know what these pagans looked like. There were many interesting questions bubbling away in her brain. Cook said they'd swapped Bessie while her ma was mangling. Why had they done that?

"When I find Bessie, I'll ask her," Alice decided. These pagans were a great mystery. But it didn't worry Alice, being caught up in a great mystery. At home, she'd lived with them all around her.

"Perk yourself up, my girl," Cook had ordered whenever she saw Alice's grave, unsmiling face. "Do you know, I feel quite perked up today," Alice decided, surprised.

She took her toast out of her pocket and crunched it. She was pretty sure it wasn't ladylike to eat toast outdoors – but, to make up for it, she kept her gloves on.

Even the lake surprised her. Today, it didn't look black and menacing. It sparkled silver in the sun. Damselflies, like blue needles, darted across it. She half-expected to find Bessie where she'd first seen her – hugging the little hill and wailing, "Let me in. Please, let me in." But there was no one on the green mound. The door was padlocked, as before.

Alice left the sugar tree, the pagan hill and the lake behind her. She was on a mission to find Bessie. She knew, vaguely, where to go. She had asked Cook last night, "Where is the gamekeeper's house?" And Cook had been very reluctant to answer. But eventually she had said: "There's a cottage in a clearing in the wood. . . But you are not meaning to go there, are you? I've warned you about that Bessie."

"Oh no," said Alice, innocently. "I was just curious."

There's a cottage in a clearing in the wood. "What will it be like?" thought Alice, as she searched every pathway. It sounded like something out of a fairy tale. She already had a picture in her head – of a charming, snug little house with a yellow thatched roof and pink roses round the door. But she had searched almost all of the woodland and she still hadn't found such a place. It was dark and piny here. Tall trees creaked over her head and shut out the light.

"This can't be right," whispered Alice, doubtfully

Here was a clearing, as Cook had described. But this cottage wasn't charming. It sulked in deep shadows. There were no roses to make it pretty. It was built of ugly, grey stone.

Even their African house had a bright sunny yard and scarlet lilies. But this house looked so gloomy, so cold. . .

"Poor Bessie," thought Alice, confused. "Surely, she doesn't live here? She likes warm places, as I do. Cold makes her bones ache."

Alice shivered, despite her warm clothes.

She hesitated. The house seemed dark and shut up – although there was smoke coming from the chimney. She didn't want to knock. There might be strangers there. And if Bessie *did* live there, she didn't want to know. It wasn't a house fit for a princess.

She took a few stumbling steps backwards.

"Ugh!" her hand touched something cold, feathery. She turned – and staggered back with her hand to her mouth. Here was a butcher's shop of dead creatures, stuck on to nails on a wooden rail. With her first horrified look, she saw a rat, a squirrel, magpies, a limp black crow—

In Africa she'd once found a thornbird's larder – he stuck his victims on thorns until he felt like a snack. She didn't know there were thornbirds in England. And this must be a very big thornbird indeed to catch squirrels and stoats. He must have a screech louder than an eagle. Claws *this* big. . . Shaking, she looked up in the tree—

"What was you doing here? Was you looking for me?

"Bessie! Where are you?"

"I ain't up in them tree-tops." And Bessie came trotting out from behind a bramble bush.

"I was looking for your English thornbird," said Alice, still fearfully scanning the trees around her. "He must be a hateful bird. Could he take a child?" At home, lots of animals took children. Leopards, wild dogs, crocodiles, that lion that took Neema's sister. They even said a python had swallowed a baby boy from the next village. Swallowed him whole.

Bessie frowned – her wrinkled face creased up even more. She squinted doubtfully and scratched at her face with her long bony fingers. "They say you come all the way from Africa..." she began, as if this accounted for Alice talking such nonsense.

"But this is the thornbird's larder," said Alice impatiently, forcing herself to look again at the sad collection of dead creatures. Some had been dead for a very long time. You couldn't tell what they'd been. They were black, withered mummies, or just scraps of fur.

"Oh!" said Bessie, her little face bright with understanding. "No!" She shook with laughter at Alice's mistake. "That's not some bird did that. What kind of bird would do that? My dad did that. It's his gamekeeper's gibbet. If he shoots or traps vermin, he hangs them up there."

"Why?" said Alice, her whirling brain shifting gears, trying to cope with this new idea, which alarmed her even more than the thought of a giant bird screeching down through the trees. "Why does your dad do that?"

"So other creatures will be warned of course," said Bessie, as if she was talking to a dim-witted child. "And not eat his game-birds' eggs. And," added Bessie, "so Mistress will know he's done his job well."

"This is a very strange country," thought Alice. "I don't know if I will *ever* get used to it."

Bessie wasn't wearing her blue canvas apron today. She was well wrapped up in an old grey shawl that crossed over and tied behind her back. She looked more like a little old grandma than ever.

"Let's go back into the sunshine," said Alice. She wanted to say, "Away from this dark, cold place. From your dad's ugly gibbet and your ugly house."

But, of course, that would be horribly rude. Which made it even more startling when Bessie spoke her thoughts for her. "It's high time them pagans came and fetched me. It's not right, is it, for a princess to live in such a *wretched* place?"

CHAPTER FIVE

"I see palaces," said Bessie dreamily, "where other folk see scummy ponds. I see gold coins where they see beans. And rich clothes where they see rags. That's how special *I* am."

Bessie and Alice were discussing pagans. By the lake, in warm sunshine, with their backs against the pagan hill.

Bessie wasn't clutching the hill and begging, "Let me in." She seemed quite resigned today about not being let inside.

"But if you can't get in," said Alice, rattling the rusty lock on the small wooden door. "Doesn't that mean *they* can't get out?"

"Ha!" said Bessie. "*They* have all sorts of magic powers. Locks are nothing to them. They make themselves invisible. They can turn themselves into eels, or adders or swans."

"Witch doctors can do that," said Alice. Then she

felt compelled to add, "Only Pa doesn't believe it, of course."

She looked out over the lake at a white swan gliding by. "Is that one of *them*?" she whispered.

"Who knows?" said Bessie. "I expect so."

"But why can't you do that," asked Alice. "If you are one of them?"

"I *will* be able to," said Bessie confidently. "I will be beautiful like them, when they take me back into their kingdom."

"Are *they* beautiful then?" asked Alice, captivated.

"Oh yes," said Bessie, eagerly. "They are like fine lords and ladies. Only they are little. Some say no bigger than a dolly. Some say they are my size. They know magic of all sorts. They have fine clothes and jewels, like your aunt has, only much finer. They have silky-smooth skin and I will be a princess there and *I* will have silky-smooth skin. And not be clumsy any more and drop plates and get called butter-fingers. In any case, I shan't have to polish jelly moulds and such any more. Goblins and elves will be my servants. They'll polish my jelly moulds for me..."

Bessie cupped her own withered-apple face in her chapped hands and dreamed about how wonderful that would be.

Alice was dreaming too. How, if she was a change-ling, her scarred back might be made smooth as silk.

Then she said to Bessie, "So you have never *seen* them then – these pagans?"

"No." Bessie shook her head, sorrowfully. "But Ma told me what they look like. Everyone here knows stories about them. Except you, of course, on account of you being from Africa... Only, you'd think they would let me see them now and then, wouldn't you?" said Bessie in a hurt voice. "Just one tiny peek. Seeing as how I am really one of them."

"How does a person know," asked Alice, trying to sound casual, "if they are a changeling?"

"Lots of ways," said Bessie. "Your mother *tells* you. She says things like: 'You're not my child. I swear you were swapped at birth.' And you *feel* it. You feel that your ma and pa aren't your real parents. That you are somebody else – a princess probably. And you *see* things, inside your head. You see beautiful crystal castles and palaces. And then you're sure you don't belong here – that you are meant to be somewhere else."

Now and again, Alice had felt some of these things. But she had to admit to herself, "Ma never said I wasn't her child."

"And look at that," said Bessie, proudly, holding up her tiny frail hand to the sun and spreading her fingers out. "If you set changelings against the sun, you can see the workings of their bodies. Look through them like glass – that's what the old stories say. We are so slight and spindly, you see."

Alice squinted into the sun at Bessie's hand. And thought she could see, well, almost see, the bones inside it. "*Eeeee*, like geckos," she said, out loud.

"Eh?" said Bessie, wrinkling her nose.

Alice shook her head. "Never mind. I was just thinking of Africa," she explained. And couldn't keep the yearning out of her voice.

Bessie drew up her bony knees and hugged them. "Ain't it terrible," she said, "not to be where you belong?"

She stroked the grassy sides of the mound. "It's lovely down there – caves all blazing with torches and silvery streams and golden castles. Oh, why don't them pagans come and get me? Why do they tease me so? I wish Ma had put me on the fire when I was little—"

"What?" said Alice. She had been gazing out over the lake, imagining the pagans' fabulous kingdom. But now she turned her startled face towards Bessie. She was deeply shocked. "What do you mean, *put you on the fire?*"

She could feel that shuddering starting, deep inside her. That old horror of flames. But Bessie said, longingly, "They did that in the olden days. If a mother thought, 'That's not my own child, that's a changeling,' she put it on the fire. And it didn't get burnt, it just flew straight up the chimney and was free—"

"*But what if it wasn't a changeling after all?*" said Alice. That shuddering was set to become a violent shaking.

Bessie gave her a puzzled look. "Its ma doesn't put it on the fire then," she said, as if it was obvious.

"You can always tell a changeling. They look like me. All little and shrivelled, with papery-thin skin and when we are babies we don't thrive. We cry all the time and—"

Alice couldn't bear any more talk of fire. She launched desperately into another subject. "That new baby – it cries and cries," she interrupted Bessie.

"What?" said Bessie, distracted for a second from talking about pagans. "The one up at the Big House? What does it look like?"

"As wrinkled as a baby baboon," said Alice, who felt she could tell Bessie the honest truth. "But don't tell Cook that. She'll say, 'I've *never*, in the whole of my life, heard such rudeness.'"

Alice did a really good imitation of Cook on her high horse. But Bessie hardly noticed. "I wonder," Bessie asked herself, thoughtfully, "if you can see through that baby when you hold it up to the light—"

"What did you say?"

"Oh, nothing," said Bessie, looking sly.

Then she seemed to get agitated again. She beat on the mound passionately with her tiny white knots of fists. She pressed her ear up against it.

"Nothing!" she said. "I can't even *hear* you. Or your music! They have lovely parties," she told Alice tearfully, "under the ground in caves big as ballrooms blazing with torches. Just picture it, Alice…"

Bessie tripped about dreamily in her big boots, being a dainty pagan lady.

Alice couldn't picture those blazing torches. It made her flinch, just trying. So she pictured those dainty pagan ladies dancing in the ballroom of Pagan Hill House. Whirling past the glittering mirrors, light as bubbles in their white, flimsy frocks.

Bessie fell on the hill and gave it another furious pounding. "Sometimes I think you've forgot all about me!" she shouted at it.

Then, quickly, she smothered her mouth with her hand. "I'd better not say that," she whispered to Alice. "It doesn't do to get on the wrong side of pagans. They can make your life a misery. They can get pretty spiteful sometimes. . ."

Alice searched for something, *anything*, comforting to say. It upset her to see Bessie so distressed. "These pagans might be fine royal lords and ladies," she thought, "who know witch doctors' magic and live in crystal castles. But they seem like cruel, teasing folk to me – not letting Bessie see them, not even for one second. . ."

Then she remembered how Bessie *could* see them – Richard's camera. "That would make her so happy," she thought. She said out loud to Bessie. "But soon you'll have a photo—"

Bessie shook her head wearily. "He won't get one – they're quick as fleas. They can make themselves invisible. Play all kinds of naughty tricks. . ."

"He has a tree-trunk mask," Alice reminded her, "and a silent shutter. He said so. He can sneak up on them. He has all the latest, most scientific things. . ."

"Huh," said Bessie, scornfully. "That won't make no difference."

Alice got up from the pagan hill. "Well, I'm going to find him. I think he's about here somewhere. I'll ask him if he has got that photo yet."

Bessie didn't stir.

"Are you staying here?" Bessie didn't answer. Her head hung down, despondently. "I'm going to find Richard then," repeated Alice. "You can mope about feeling sorry for yourself if you want to."

At last Bessie lifted her head. "If you see a lion," she told Alice. "Don't be afraid. He won't hurt you. He's only one of the statues."

"Huh," said Alice, scornfully. Then plunged off into the trees.

She found Richard quite easily. He was setting up his camera, on its spindly tripod legs, alongside a hedge.

"Shhh," he told her. "There's a spotted flycatcher in here, feeding her chicks..."

He rummaged around in his big canvas bag of photography gear.

His mind was totally fixed on getting his picture. He seemed to have forgotten their disastrous first meeting. Alice hadn't forgotten yesterday's shocks – the tree-trunk mask, the magnesium flash, the stone lion – but she too had her mind on a picture. Nothing else mattered to her, at this moment, but that Bessie should get her photo.

So she gulped down her wariness and said, straight out, "Did you take the picture then?"

"Eh?" Richard swivelled his head to stare at her, his face one big question mark.

"The photo you promised Bessie," Alice urged eagerly. "The one of the pagans?"

"Ahhh." Richard's mind was rapidly clicking over. He seemed to see her, this strange, sallow-skinned girl, for the first time. He was nervous with girls. In fact, he hardly knew any, except for his cousins. But he was instantly interested, caught up in her excitement. Especially as it involved his latest craze, photography.

"You haven't taken it yet, have you?" Alice accused him.

Her awkwardness with English boys, the English rules of politeness – this time, even they couldn't stop her. She was speaking now in her own natural voice. With her own, natural feelings bursting through. She'd hardly done that since she came here. And when she *had* risked it, it had mostly got her into trouble. The only person she'd been free-and-easy with was Bessie. She would break any rules to get this photo, for Bessie's sake.

"You said you could do it," Alice reminded Richard.

"So I can," he said, nodding. Then he told her, "Come to my house this afternoon. At three o'clock."

"Where is your house?" A twinge of nervousness gripped her. Alice had never been off her uncle's estate, except with company. This would be her very first journey alone in England. She felt like a bold explorer.

"It's just down the road, on the village green," said Richard. "A red house, with a big mess of ivy on the front."

He almost added, "*Everyone* knows the doctor's house."

But then he remembered that this girl was not everyone. She was a visitor from a strange land. Richard was interested in Africa. He'd read adventure stories in *Boy's Own* magazine, about exploring and shooting lions and fighting off savage tribesmen. He was keen to ask her all about it.

But she would keep on about *that* photograph.

"Can I bring Bessie?" she asked.

Richard liked Bessie. She was amusing. He felt sorry for her because she'd been born simple-minded and wrongly made-up, like some wizened, elfin creature. But a gamekeeper's idiot daughter, just a kid, coming to visit him at *his* house? The idea nearly made him laugh out loud. What would his friends at school say, if they ever found out? But he reminded himself that Alice didn't know yet how things were done here.

"No, better not," was all he replied. "You can come to my house, though."

She was all right. She wasn't at all stuck-up. But it wouldn't have surprised him if she'd said, "No, I'm not allowed." She could easily have looked down her nose at a village doctor's son, because her uncle was rich and a great soldier.

But Alice, who didn't know she should be looking down her nose at anyone, simply said, "I shall be there this afternoon then."

She turned to go away. Best leave him alone, she thought, if he was going to stalk those pagans and snatch a photo for Bessie. She'd already learned that pagans were teasers and tricksters. They had magical powers. They could shape-shift, make themselves disappear into thin air. He would need to be cunning – and quick.

But Richard called something after her. "What are pagans supposed to look like? I suppose they are sweet little things, are they?" he asked her, remembering the pictures of fairies he'd seen in his small cousin Mildred's books. "With fluttery wings?"

Alice frowned. She couldn't remember anything about wings, fluttery or otherwise. And "sweet" seemed hardly the word to describe them. They were splendid creatures certainly. But they could be cruel and selfish. Deep in her heart, Alice didn't entirely trust these pagans to do right by Bessie and take her back to be a royal princess. What would Bessie do if they *had* forgotten her? And she was stuck, for the rest of her life, in that withered body in that cold, dreary cottage? Polishing rich folk's jelly moulds when she should, by rights, be waited upon hand, foot and finger? It didn't bear thinking about.

"Just so I will recognize one when it crosses my camera lens..." Richard further explained, to shake Alice out of her long silence.

Alice tried to gather up in her mind all the facts she knew about pagans. Facts Bessie had learned from the old stories. But then she couldn't help adding a few inventions of her own.

"Pagan ladies have fine clothes with long, flowing dresses and they are beautiful and proud and elegant," she told Richard. "They are like English queens, only tinier." She added, as a serious afterthought, "How tiny I do not know."

She couldn't understand why Richard kept grinning. She hoped he was taking this photo seriously. It meant the world to Bessie.

"I forgot," said Alice, "pagan ladies – they have perfect skin, as smooth as a marble statue."

"That's just the ticket!" said Richard, snapping his fingers as if he was suddenly inspired.

Alice's heart sank a little. It was just as she'd feared. English young ladies should have lovely, clear, rose-petal skin. Even boys thought they should have. She pictured her own back and those thick, ropy scars. But she didn't waste any pity on herself – apart from one tiny, sad sigh.

"I'll get Bessie a picture of a pagan lady," said Richard, with a business-like nod of his head. "I can absolutely guarantee it."

Alice was impressed. He seemed very confident. "I'll see you at three o'clock then," she said and hurried back to tell Bessie the good news. As she rushed through the woods she composed in her head what she was going to say. It began with, "Cheer up, Bessie. You shall have your picture this very afternoon. . ."

There was the pagan hill with its wooden door, as small as a door in a hen house. But Bessie had gone. For one wild moment, Alice thought, "Those pagans have finally gone and done it. They've taken her in." But then she saw that the rusty padlock hadn't been touched.

She shook her head, "No, she's just wandered off."

She was sad for Bessie – but glad for herself because she still had her friend. It had already occurred to her that, when Bessie took her rightful place as a pagan princess, she might be too high-and-mighty to speak to mere humans.

Alice thought once about seeking Bessie out. Perhaps she'd gone home to the gamekeeper's cottage? But she didn't think twice about it. Here the lake glittered, a kingfisher flashed blue in the sun. She didn't feel like going back into the dark pines. Or seeing that gruesome gibbet of poor, dead creatures.

"I'll find her later," Alice decided. "When I have that photo, here, in my hands."

It would be better to wait, she told herself. Despite his confidence, she still wasn't totally sure that Richard could snap this photo. Even with his Thornton and Pickard's silent shutter and the latest Dallmeyer lens. Like African witches and sprites and goblins, these English pagans had been here for a very long time. They were ancient, older than mountains, perhaps older than time itself. It needed a very clever human to get the better of them.

When Alice went back to Pagan Hill House, there was a terrible fuss about something. As she slipped in by the scullery door, she could hear people yelling.

Her first thought was, "Oh no. That baby has died." Then, "Perhaps Aunt Evaline has died."

But she realized the commotion came from the linen room. It was Bertha on the rampage.

"I should have known you'd be hiding in here," Bertha was thundering at someone, in her mooing, slow-talking voice.

"If a cow could talk it would talk like that," thought Alice, as she moved closer.

"What was you up to just now?" Bertha bellowed. "You shouldn't go front of house. Let alone upstairs, into the nursery. What was you thinking of, my girl?"

The other voice, half snivelling, half defiant, answered, "I wanted to see that new baby—"

"Nurse said you *picked him up*!" Bertha's shock was so great she could barely force out the words.

"I didn't, I didn't, I didn't," the other voice protested frantically. "I weren't doing nothing. I was only peeping into his crib."

It was Bessie, of course. Alice had known in her bones it would be. Bessie getting told off, as usual. Only this time not for breaking plates, or letting the pagans make off with the kitchen utensils. This time she had done something much more serious. She had gone the other side of the green baize doors. She had gone *upstairs*. When her place was down in the kitchen polishing pans and jelly moulds.

Alice knew those rules by now – where servants should be and where they shouldn't. And she knew Bessie was in frightful trouble.

She thought, trembling, "Bessie will lose her place."

Then she thought, in a flash, of a way to rescue her. The very idea of it made her stomach clench, tight as a walnut. She reminded herself, "You have touched a chameleon and lived." That made her feel bolder, as if she had a charmed life.

She pushed open the linen room door and walked into the heat and the smell of fresh laundry.

Bertha, in her crackling black head housemaid's dress, towered over Bessie. Bessie was pressed up against the pipes. She looked tiny and shrunken beside big, bony Bertha.

"*Cockroach*," thought Alice, out of the blue. "*Red scuttling cockroach with wavy legs.*" That made her grin, she couldn't help it. And she noticed, for the first time, that Bertha had grey hairs sprouting from a mole on her chin.

"What do you find so funny, Miss?" asked Bertha. But her voice had softened. She could not be as rude to one of the family, even a charity case from Africa, as she could be to Bessie.

"I heard what you said," Alice told Bertha, trying to keep her voice calm and ladylike. "And I have come to tell you that *I* sent Bessie upstairs. On an errand for me. She must have lost her way, that's all."

Bertha looked immediately suspicious. "Oh dear," thought Alice. "She isn't as stupid as I thought she was."

"What errand would that be, Miss?" demanded Bertha, sharply.

Bessie wriggled against the hot pipes, warming her skinny bottom. There was no help coming from her. Alice searched frantically in her brain for an answer. *"What errand? What errand?"*

She took a deep breath. "I sent her to fetch my corset."

"Your corset, Miss?" repeated Bertha, goggle-eyed.

"Yes, Bertha," said Alice, with perfect politeness. "You know I have just come from Africa and everything is new here and I'm still trying to learn the rules. Well, I went out without my corset. I thought, 'Silly me, I've clean forgot to put it on!' So I sent Bessie back to find it – but she mistook the room. It's not her fault."

To Alice's amazement, Bertha seemed to swallow the story about the corset. As if nothing this strange, foreign child did could surprise her.

"Well," she said sniffily, "we'll let it go at that, I suppose – but Bessie had no business in the nursery. Let alone to pick the baby up!" she added, outraged all over again.

"She said she didn't," Alice pointed out, coolly.

"She had no business upstairs at all," said Bertha stiffly. "Even on errands for you. Please remember that in future, Miss." She bustled out, her black dress crackling.

"Phew, that was lucky," whistled Bessie. "That hateful old cow was hopping mad. Did you see her? I'd like to give her a good boot!" Bessie's tiny face screwed up alarmingly.

"I wouldn't spoil good boot leather," shrugged Alice. "Just turn her into a beetle. Then she might fall in a po and drown."

"*Ha, ha, ha!*" Bessie's hoots of laughter startled Alice. Bessie clutched her skinny body and rocked helplessly to and fro. "*Ha, ha ha!*"

"Bessie, shut up, you idiot," said Alice, dragging her by the arm. "Do you want to start a riot?"

They hid out in the glasshouse, like two conspirators. "I'm not supposed to be in here neither," said Bessie, looking around. "I'll catch it if the gardener comes in. It's nice in here though, ain't it? Nice and warm. With such lovely flowers..."

Alice nodded. She took a great sniff of the hot, lily-scented air. "This reminds me of Africa," she told Bessie. "My ma planted red lilies just like these outside our house."

Bessie looked curiously at Alice. Her little goblin face became suddenly deeply concerned. She peered into Alice's eyes. "Are you *unbearably* homesick?" she asked, as if it was a new idea that had just occurred to her. One of her frail, doll-like hands crept over Alice's hand and patted it.

"Not *unbearably*," said Alice, because after all, she had woken up that morning determined to make the best of things. "But quite a lot." Then she couldn't help herself adding. "But won't you miss your ma and pa when you go to live with the pagans?"

"They're not my *real* ma and pa though," Bessie reminded her. "My real ma and pa are a king and queen. He is so handsome and she is so beautiful," said Bessie dreamily. "And my *royal* ma wouldn't be seen dead mangling of course," added Bessie. "She has servants to do all that for her."

Alice's next question had been troubling her for some time. She knew she could speak her real thoughts to Bessie. But even so, she asked the question gently, in case Bessie was upset.

"Why did your royal ma and pa give you away to humans, Bessie?"

Bessie was not distressed, or even put out. "It is because they cared about me," she answered, without the slightest delay. "Pagans ain't very good at looking after their own babies. . ."

Alice could imagine that – they probably left them all over the place. Forgot to feed and change them when they were having parties, riding through the night sky on white horses, or out borrowing jelly moulds and such like.

"So," continued Bessie, "they give 'em to humans to look after properly. Especially if they were born sickly like me. Why, there are changelings all over the place—"

"When they take you back," interrupted Alice, "will they put back your ma and pa's real daughter in your place?"

"Oh yes," said Bessie, as if it was obvious. "And Ma and Pa will like her much better than they like me. They will be glad to get rid of me. They don't really like me at all. Ma says, 'What did we do to deserve you?'"

Alice didn't want to think about Bessie going. Why, they had only just become friends. She wondered if she would like Bessie's human replacement as much as she liked Bessie. "I don't think I will," thought Alice doubtfully. "In fact, I'm sure I won't."

"I am homesick like you," said Bessie, her little face twisted up with grief. "And no wonder. When them dratted pagans make me wait and wait. I should have been a princess long ago. I am sick of it sometimes, I am," she wailed.

This was the perfect chance to ask the other important question that rattled around in Alice's brain. She wanted to ask Bessie "*Why* don't your royal ma and pa come and claim you for their own? *Why* do they leave you here?"

But, even though there was plain speaking between them, she didn't dare ask it. "If I were a changeling," thought Alice, "I would wonder why they never came."

How did Bessie keep such unshakeable faith when those pagans let her down time after time? "I don't know whether *I* would be able to," thought Alice. "Unless I had a photograph of course. That would help."

So, instead of asking awkward questions, she found herself comforting Bessie "*Shush, shush!*" as if she were calming a distressed baby. "Bessie, listen," she urged her. "I've got some good news to give you about those pagans. Guess what it is? Richard is taking that photograph for you. You know, the one he promised. I'm to meet him this afternoon."

Alice guessed that Bessie's face would change in an instant, like the sun coming out from behind storm clouds. And it did. Bessie was radiant.

"I can't hardly believe it," she cried. "I will be able to see them at last!"

"I don't know whether it will be a photo of your regal parents, the king and queen," Alice cautioned her. "I think that would be too much to hope for, don't you?"

"I suppose you're right," said Bessie, a tiny bit regretfully. But then she bounced back, as delighted as ever. "It don't matter though. So long as it is a pagan." Her face fell again, became suddenly serious. "After all," she reminded Alice. "I have never even seen *one* of them."

"Well, you shall see one before today is over." said Alice. "Perhaps a whole crowd of them." It was Alice's great desire to see her new friend happy. She knew how sad and bewildering it felt when you didn't belong. But even as she was promising Bessie the moon and stars, little warning bells were tinkling away in her brain.

"Richard didn't actually *swear* he would have the photo," she told herself sternly. "What if no pagans cross his camera lens? It may take him weeks to find one."

She didn't know how Bessie would bear the disappointment. She decided to change the subject quickly, so as not to get Bessie's hopes up too much.

"By the way," she said, not much caring, "what were you doing upstairs in the nursery just now, picking Aunt Evaline's baby up?"

"Trying to hold him up against the sun, to see if I could see through him," replied Bessie. She seemed astounded that Alice should need to ask.

"And could you?" said Alice, intrigued – but baffled.

"No." said Bessie. "There was heavy velvet curtains keeping the sunshine out. That room is fearful dark. I couldn't hardly see him. But you said he was a changeling, didn't you?"

"Did I?" Alice frowned. She couldn't remember saying that.

"Only if he is," Bessie pointed out, "he'll need someone to help him." She stuck out her small pointy chin and nodded hard. "If I'd had someone to help me, I'd be in my crystal castle now, eating bread and treacle."

"Bread and treacle?" grinned Alice. "That's not very grand."

"I know," said Bessie, rubbing her tiny stomach and burping. "But it's what I *crave*!"

Alice laughed out loud then, a hearty belly laugh. Cut short by the gruff voice of the gardener, "Eh, 'oo's in my 'ot 'ouse?" Then his slow, heavy tread on the gravel.

"I'm off," said Bessie, scampering out.

Alice followed her, out of the stifling heat into the cold, blowy wind. Across the cobbled yard and into the scullery passage, with the gardener bellowing indignantly behind them.

The scullery passage smelled of fresh-cut cucumbers. "Is it teatime already?" thought Alice, dismayed. She had no watch of her own. She had no idea so many hours had passed. "I am late for Richard's then!"

Bessie, of course, had no idea of the time either.

"I'll wait for you by the pagan hill," said Bessie. "Until you come back and bring me that photo."

Alice worried again that she had promised too much. "I'm not sure when I will be back," she warned.

"Don't matter," said Bessie. She peeped out of the scullery door. "That pig of a gardener has gone," she reported back to Alice. And then Bessie was gone too. But not before she had clasped Alice's hand and said, nodding her head fervently, "I *will* wait."

Cook's beady eye glared at Alice as she rushed through the kitchen.

"You are nearly late for lunch, Miss," she said.

"Lunch?" said Alice, confused all over again. "I smelled cucumbers so I thought it was three o'clock."

Cook shook her head sorrowfully. She said nothing – just carried on slicing up cucumbers to put on the lunchtime cold salmon. But Alice could make a pretty good guess what she might be thinking. "My Lord! How can one even *begin* to civilize such a child? That tells the time *by smell*?"

But Alice was pleased she had mistaken the time. It meant she had some hours spare to get ready. This was a very important occasion – her first visit, alone, to an English home. It felt like sitting an examination. She would have to behave correctly. She would have to watch herself every second.

"If it wasn't for Bessie," she decided. "I would have told Richard, 'No, I'm not allowed to come.'"

But Bessie was waiting on the pagan hill. There was no way out of it now.

Alice's heart was fluttering again, like butterflies in a sunny clearing. But it surprised her that, this time, it wasn't just nerves. Somewhere, deep inside, she felt excited as well.

Up in her bedroom, she did the best she could. She couldn't make that yellowy skin pink and blushing. "But I don't want to look a fright either," she thought. So she brushed her hair neatly with the silver-backed hairbrush. She even put on that corset, though it felt tight as a drum skin and rubbed at her scars. Finally, she kitted herself out in hat, coat and gloves. She checked herself critically in her dressing table mirror. To her amazement it showed her ... one well-brought-up English young lady, ready for visiting!

"Just watch your manners," she warned her reflection in the mirror. "And don't give yourself away."

CHAPTER SIX

Alice walked self-consciously down the road and into the village. She didn't actually see them – but she felt certain that eyes were spying on her. "There's that charity case come all the way from Africa. Watch. She's sure to disgrace herself." Alice tried to hold her head high and defiant like an African princess.

"*Cockroaches*," she murmured viciously, in time to her clumping boots. "*Cockroaches, cockroaches, cockroaches.*"

But none of those charms worked. When she was crossing the green, ringed by houses, it felt as scary as leopards circling her in the bush. Even though this was just a sleepy English village, she could feel the hairs prickling at the back of her neck...

Then she stubbed her boot on a stone, stumbled, almost pitched straight on to her nose. She braced herself for howls of laughter from somewhere. She could hardly believe it when there was nothing but silence. She dared to look round her. No one was on the green.

"Where are they all?" she wondered. "I know. They're probably in their parlours, taking after-noon tea."

She could have bolted, there and then, before she made any more mistakes. Only the thought of the photo, and Bessie, waiting full of hope on the pagan hill, kept her walking on.

Bessie had to have *someone* on her side. Cook wasn't; Bertha certainly wasn't. Even Bessie's ma and pa didn't seem to want her much. And those pagans – they should have been on Bessie's side, more than anyone. But Alice knew, from African tales, that creatures like pagans can't be trusted. They aren't human. You should approach them with extreme caution. Actually, it's best to mind your own business and not approach them at all.

"Bessie's a pagan too," Alice reminded herself. "And you trust her."

But it was no good. She couldn't think of Bessie as one hundred per cent pagan. Bessie had spent too long among humans, like a wild cat that's been half tamed.

Red bricks, swags of dark-green ivy. Was this the doctor's house at last? Yes, here was a shiny brass plate by the front door that told you so.

Alice gulped once, twice, pulled on her gloves more firmly, then tugged at the bell. She could hear its solemn DING DONG, deep inside the house.

Nobody came. The door stayed firmly shut against her. Alice stood there, embarrassed, trying not to wriggle her shoulders. "My back's itching something cruel," she thought, grimacing.

Did a curtain twitch in the next-door house? Every house on the green had a good view of her, ringing and ringing at the doctor's bell and not being allowed in. She had a sudden, panicky notion. What if Richard only invited her for a joke? What if they were all in on it? Perhaps the whole village was crouched behind its net curtains, having a good laugh at her humiliation –

She couldn't bear it a second longer. Frantic to hide herself, she ducked down the side of the doctor's house and found herself in a back garden, stuffed full of bushes and trees. At least here she seemed to be alone. She ripped off her gloves and spread her cramped fingers.

"I *hate* this place!" she told the trees. She didn't have a spear to shake, or a shield to rattle it against. But she could yell like a warrior. So she did. It just came exploding out of her, "YAAAA!" Then her hand flew to smother her mouth, in case anyone had heard that most unladylike noise. Someone had – because a muffled voice enquired: "Who's out there?"

Alice whipped round. She thrust aside some bendy stems and found herself staring at a wooden wall.

"Is that you, Richard?" she said, puzzled, still searching. "Where are you? I can't find you."

"I'm in the old potting shed."

71

Alice found a door, pushed at it. There was something inside; it seemed to be blocking her way—

"No!" commanded an urgent voice. "Don't come in yet."

Alice dropped the latch as if it was red-hot. She fell back, upset all over again. She was already thinking: "What have I done wrong now? Why aren't I allowed in?" when the voice in the shed explained, "The light will ruin the picture. Wait a couple of minutes, will you?"

"The picture," thought Alice. "He must mean Bessie's picture." Instantly, she forgot her own hurt feelings. "Have you really managed to take one?" she called out excitedly.

But the voice in the shed was already speaking about something else.

"I'm sorry I wasn't in the house to let you in. I forgot – it's the housekeeper's day off. I'm shocking rude, I know. It comes of having no mother to teach me manners."

"Pardon?" said Alice, pressing an ear up against the wooden planks.

"I said, MY MOTHER IS DEAD AND I'VE GOT NO MANNERS."

Alice jumped back from the door, startled. She could think of nothing to say. She'd been well scolded by Cook for speaking her honest thoughts about death. But even to her it seemed disrespectful, discussing someone's dead ma through a potting shed wall.

So she waited, nervously chewing her nails. There was silence from inside the shed. She wondered if Richard had forgotten her. Then he called out, "You can come in now."

She had to fight her way in. There seemed to be a blanket covering the door. A ruby lamp, hooked to a shelf, gave the only light. The strong stink of chemicals almost made her choke.

Richard was sitting on an old trunk, hunched over a bench crammed with trays and bottles and rubber tubes. He said, without looking up, "Do you want to see Bessie's photograph?" Alice was desperate to see it but she had something to get out of the way first. "Sorry about your ma," she gasped.

"What?" said Richard, turning his head to stare at her, his face bathed in a hellish red glow. "That's no matter," he said. Then contradicted himself with a flurry of headshaking. "No, I don't mean it's *no matter*. I mean that Mother died when I was born. So I am used to it."

"Oh," nodded Alice, weak with relief that she hadn't offended.

Richard was concentrating again on what he was doing. "Look," he said, budging up on the trunk so she could sit down beside him.

She saw a glass plate being swished around in a tray.

"Here goes," said Richard eagerly. "Here's the picture coming." Alice peered through the dim red light, at the glass plate in the fixing bath. She saw a milky image on the glass. It became clearer. There were dark stains, grey patches.

"What is it?" she said, feeling horribly let down. "I can't make head nor tail of it. It's just a jumble."

"It's the negative." Richard lifted out the glass plate and plunged it into the washing tank. "Wait, it's going to be a good picture, I can tell. I'll take the plate out and let it dry a few minutes. Then I'll print it on paper. And you'll see everything clear."

They waited, squashed together in the cramped, dark space, for the negative to dry.

"Is this proper?" thought Alice, shuffling aside to make a bigger space between them. "I'm sure there are rules about this."

But Richard didn't seem to care if their bodies were touching. He was busy reaching out for equipment, finding it even on dark shelves, outside the burning red circle of the ruby lamp.

Beside him, Alice coughed. She felt sick; the sulphur reek made her head spin. Their faces and the bench-top seemed to smoulder eerily... She glanced down at her red hands, resting on the bench. "I'm on fire," thought Alice, suddenly. "My hands are on fire!"

A bombshell of terrible panic burst in her brain. She sprang up, tore the blanket aside, yanked the door open and fell out into fresh air. She gulped in great lungfuls of it, staggering round, waving her hands wildly to beat out the flames. Then she saw there were no flames. Her skin was not blistering and bubbling. She didn't feel any pain. She slumped down in a heap in the long grass. The red mist dissolved from her eyes.

"You silly little fool," her sensible voice started to nag her. "What have you done? You've ruined Bessie's picture now. You've let the light in the shed."

For the door was wide open. And Richard was standing in it, looking aghast.

She began straightaway to apologize. "Sorry, sorry—" But Richard apologized first. "I must get more ventilation," he said. "Those chemicals – Dad's always warning me – they even make *me* feel faint and dizzy."

"The picture," Alice begged him. "Tell me quickly, is it spoiled?"

Richard looked mystified. "Spoiled? No fear. At any rate, I don't think so. Look, stay here, and I'll print it out for you. It'll only take a few minutes."

He disappeared inside the potting shed, closing the door.

Alice stayed on the ground for a bit. She felt weak with the after-shock and with relief that she hadn't spoiled the picture. Then she got up, dusted some bright yellow pollen off her coat.

"You great booby," she told herself.

She felt ashamed that she'd lost control so badly. It wasn't what well-brought up English girls did. "*Eeeee*, it's high time you stopped all this nonsense," she lectured herself. "You can't stay afraid of fire *all* your life."

At least Richard hadn't guessed the truth – her scarred back was still a secret. Those old burns ached worse than ever at the moment. She tried hard to ignore them.

Richard came bursting out of the shed: "I think this is the best picture I ever took," he told her. "I used an Ilford Chromatic plate. It's sharp as sharp, isn't it?"

Anxiously, Alice peered at Bessie's picture. It was on paper now, a proper photo. "Careful, it's still a bit damp," warned Richard.

She couldn't believe her eyes. There, just as Richard had said, sharp as sharp, was a pagan lady.

"See," said Richard excitedly. "See how I did it? Clever, ain't it?"

Alice stared at the picture, greedily taking in every detail. The background was strange, like tree bark. The pagan lady had her slim, white arms flung up, as if she was trying to escape.

"I see!" cried Alice, thrilled. "I see how you did it. I must tell Bessie. You sugared the tree, didn't you? What an awfully clever thing to do. You caught her like a butterfly, so you could take her picture. Did you use your silent shutter? I expect she didn't even know she was being snapped. She wasn't hurt at all, was she? Did you let her go, straight after?"

Richard nodded his head, dumbly.

In fact, the little pagan didn't look in the least bit bothered. Her creamy arms were flung up, as if she was about to flee. But her tiny oval face was smooth, her eyes were blank. No sign of alarm or distress clouded them. She was as perfect as a snowdrop.

"She looks quite cold and haughty, doesn't she?" said Alice. "But that's pagans for you, they're a toffee-nosed lot. Mind you, they don't need to fawn upon us humans..."

Richard didn't reply; he seemed to have lost his tongue. But Alice was too delighted with the photo to notice.

She had smooth, satiny skin, this lady, and long flowing tresses. Her dress was high-class and elegant – a simple, draped gown, that left her arms bare. It showed off her lovely neck. "Perfect for parties," thought Alice.

She was captivated by this tiny pagan princess – for she had made up her mind she was a princess. She was fizzing with things to say. She hadn't talked so much since she came to England.

"We know how big pagans are now," she told Richard. "About the size of a child's doll, would you say? Only Bessie was never quite sure. Thank you, thank you, thank you for this photo."

She flung a friendly arm round Richard's neck, as she would with Mayamiko or Neema. "Eeee, it's a wonderful photo. You're a little gem, Richard, really you are—"

"Errr." Richard seemed stunned. He could barely speak. He just stared at her, disbelief and dismay on his face.

"Oh dear, I expect I shouldn't have hugged him." thought Alice, hastily dropping her arm. "Or called him a little gem. I've probably broken about one hundred rules."

But she didn't have time now to fret about that. The photo was all she could think about.

It was better than she'd ever dared hope. A real live pagan princess – caught for an instant by the sugar tree. And for ever by Richard's camera.

"Can you make others of these?" she asked Richard, eagerly. "From that glass thing?"

"What, from the negative?" said Richard, who still seemed shaken. "Er, yes, as many as you like. If you feel up to it."

"I'm fine now," said Alice. "Those chemicals just made me awful dizzy."

She didn't relish going back into the potting shed – into that fiery red glow and that rotten egg smell. But this time it was just about bearable. Richard had switched off the red light. He'd unshuttered the window and let in daylight and fresh air. She sat down again on the old trunk.

"All I need is some more bromide paper," began Richard. "Then I'll have to make the shed dark again."

And, as he reached out, with a quick jerk of his arm, he somehow managed to sweep the negative on to the floor. The glass plate cracked and fell into four pieces.

"What did you do that for?" asked Alice, appalled.

"I didn't do it on purpose. It was an accident."

Richard bent down to gather up the biggest pieces, tried to fit them together like a jigsaw. Then shrugged, defeated. It was useless – the negative was ruined. "It's finished," he said. "I can't print any more pictures from it now."

Alice couldn't believe he'd been so clumsy, when he seemed so nimble-fingered before. But it wasn't a hopeless disaster.

"At least we've got one print," she said, brightly. "And Bessie will have the picture she always wanted."

And she put the photo, made more precious now because it was the only one in existence, carefully into her coat pocket.

CHAPTER SEVEN

On the way back to Aunt Evaline's, Alice took the photo out of her coat pocket a dozen times to look at it.

"Bessie will be tickled pink," she thought.

But, as she gazed at the strange, wild, little pagan princess, trapped by the sugar tree, she began to have thoughts that shocked her – that seemed to betray her friend Bessie. But she just couldn't help herself.

"If I give this to Bessie she won't keep it secret. She won't be able to keep her mouth shut."

She would tell the whole world about the pagans, show the photo to everyone she met. And the world would come flocking to see them. They would paw over the photo, come gawping through the woodland. The pagans would never be left in peace.

"And that'll be that," thought Alice. "No more pagans. They will up sticks and move somewhere else."

They'd have to abandon their ancient underground kingdom, where they'd lived for thousands of years.

Their crystal castles and golden palaces would be empty of music and feasting. They would crumble into dust.

She began to think, seriously, about not giving the photo to Bessie but keeping it herself.

"It's for Bessie's own good," she thought.

She walked back to Aunt Evaline's arguing with herself, this way, that way. And all the while she knew that Bessie was waiting on the pagan hill for the photo she had in her pocket.

She almost went to give it to her. She knew how much it meant to Bessie, to hold this photo in her hands, to see it with her own eyes. She knew she would be broken-hearted if she didn't get it. But then she took out the photo and looked at the beautiful pagan princess again.

"It would be too cruel to give Bessie this photo," Alice persuaded herself. "When those pagans tease her so much and never come. It would be kinder not to. It would just get her hopes up too much."

She'd made her final decision. She turned away from the wood, tucked the photograph into her coat and headed for the Big House.

Cook was in the kitchen, with flour up to her elbows, whacking pastry with a rolling pin.

Alice smiled back politely as Cook glared at her.

"Where have you been all this time, Miss?" huffed Cook. "Lucky your Aunt Evaline has been asleep, or you'd have to account for yourself."

But, this time, Cook couldn't make Alice feel unwanted, or like a freakish outsider. Cook had lived here all her life but she had never been chosen to see a pagan.

"I've seen one," thought Alice. "This is probably the only photograph in the world. And it's here, inside my coat." It made her feel very special.

Richard had seen a pagan too, with his own eyes. He'd trapped one on the sugar tree. But somehow that didn't count. It wasn't pagans Richard cared about, but photography. Pagans didn't seem to interest him – he could take them or leave them.

But Alice was mightily interested in pagans. For the first time since she came here, she felt truly involved. She was learning important things about England – not just fussy old rules about gloves and corsets. She was uncovering deep, dark, magical mysteries. Secret things, that even Cook and Bertha didn't know about, didn't have eyes to see. Even though they'd lived here all their lives, with pagans right under their noses.

She couldn't help teasing Cook a little, just to get her own back.

"I've been thinking about these pagans," she said, trying to look humble..

Cook clucked irritably. She squeezed some pastry into a fat, white snake, "You should be thinking about tidying your hair," she grumbled, "in time for supper."

"What do you think they look like, Cook?" asked Alice, smiling her most grateful smile.

Cook's voice grew less harsh. She was pleased to see Alice so respectful. "Oh they are horrid things. Horrid," she answered. "As bothersome as wasps. They are on very bad terms with humans. They *say* if a human wants to deal with them, he must protect himself. Because they're such flighty things; they can be nice – or turn nasty at the drop of a hat. You never know where you are with pagans."

Alice hadn't meant to ask Cook any more questions. But she couldn't stop herself. "How does a human being protect himself against pagans – in case they turn nasty?"

Cook had lost patience. "All these questions! These creatures, they are just make-believe you know. Just silly stories."

"But how *does* he?" persisted Alice.

"Oh, I don't know, Miss. The old stories say you must carry iron and salt. Pagans hate those. And turn your coat inside-out, if you please! Don't ask me why. But I've no time for all this nonsense. I've got pies to make."

Alice slipped away, up to her bedroom, frowning thoughtfully.

Watching herself in the mirror, she brushed her hair one hundred times with the silver-backed brush. She tried not to think about Bessie. Was she waiting on the pagan mound? She couldn't still be there, surely? It would be getting dark soon.

She thought instead about Richard. She did like him. Of course, with her back, there was no point in daydreaming. She sighed and gazed at the photo of the lovely pagan princess, with her perfect skin. Skin so lustrous and smooth it seemed like polished marble. Bessie should look like that, thought Alice. Instead she was trapped in the wrong body. Poor, butter-fingers Bessie with her big boots and loud, rough voice coming out of that tiny, withered-apple face.

"It's a tragedy," thought Alice, gravely. "It's just not fair. Those pagans shouldn't be allowed to get away with it. I wish I could do *something* to help her. She should have what's rightly hers. She shouldn't have to suffer like she does."

But Alice couldn't see any way to make those pagans do what they ought.

After supper, she was summoned by Nurse to see Aunt Evaline. Her aunt, Alice was relieved to see, looked loads better. She was still in bed. But now she wore a very stylish bed jacket and her hair was sleek and glossy.

"She doesn't look at all like Ma," Alice decided. That single thought about Ma really shocked her. It made her realize that she hadn't been homesick for Ma or Pa once, not for hours and hours.

"I'm so sorry, my dear," said Aunt Evaline, raising herself up from her lacy pillows. "You've been dreadfully neglected. I'll make it up to you as soon as I'm up and about again, I promise. But have you been amusing yourself?"

"Oh yes," said Alice, nodding. "Don't worry about me. I've been amusing myself pretty well."

She took a polite interest in the new baby before she went out. "What's his name to be?" she asked Aunt Evaline, as she leaned over his crib.

"I think we shall call him William," said Aunt Evaline.

William looked less like a wrinkled baby baboon today. In fact, he was beginning to look quite plump. You definitely wouldn't be able to see through *him* if you held him up to the light. "I'm *sure* he's not a changeling," thought Alice, scratching her ear. He'd stopped wailing all the time. He gurgled and waved his arms about when you tickled his chin. Alice was beginning to think that Bessie didn't really know much about pagans. If she did, she wouldn't see changelings round every corner.

"I think changelings are as rare as hens' teeth," decided Alice. "*And* I think I'm better acquainted with pagans than Bessie is, even though she's supposed to be one."

It was no good begging pagans, "Take me in! Take me in!" Pleading didn't work with them. Bessie had pleaded for years and wept buckets. And where had it got her? You had to stand up to them. And you had to have something they wanted.

Then a plan, a plan so bold it made her gasp, began to assemble itself in Alice's mind.

She told everyone she saw – Cook, Nurse, Bertha, Aunt Evaline – that she was going to bed early. "I can't keep my eyes open," she told them, with a huge, sleepy yawn. But later that evening, she tiptoed down the back stairs and slipped out of the house by the scullery door.

Before she left she went searching in the kitchen. It was empty, washed by blue moonlight. The big copper pans and jelly moulds glimmered like dull gold. Alice opened a few drawers and cupboards.

"This will do," she thought, choosing a small, cast-iron frying-pan that Cook used to make omelettes in. She tried stuffing it into her coat pocket. It wouldn't fit; she decided she'd have to carry it. She picked up the salt cellar and poured salt into her pocket instead. It trickled out maddeningly slowly. She frowned, unscrewed the top and dumped the entire contents into her pocket: "Better be safe than sorry," she told herself.

Then, as last precaution, she took off her coat and put it back on again, inside out.

Alice was going to play a hazardous game tonight. She meant to take matters into her own hands – she meant to try and bargain with pagans.

She wasn't entirely unprepared. She was protected with iron and salt and an inside-out coat. And she had all her African experience to call on. Those stories she knew so well – about tricky spirits and treacherous wizards and crafty magicians – had taught her one thing. For mere humans, dealing with creatures like pagans is a very risky business.

"But I have as good a chance as anyone," she thought. Probably better. She'd walked calmly towards a witch light; she'd touched a chameleon and lived. She'd been stalked in the bush by something with golden eyes and survived.

Surely she could outwit these English pagans – who seemed to be a sort of watered-down version of all those African dangers?

But she was ready for anything, just in case, as Cook said, they turned nasty. She patted her bulging pocket, to reassure herself she had enough salt. Took her frying-pan in her hand like a knight takes his sword. And set off.

The wood was creepy, trembling with moonlight. She stroked the friendly stone lion's pug nose, so she didn't lose her nerve. "Wish me luck," she whispered. As she left him behind she felt suddenly vulnerable and alone. A stick cracked under her boots – she felt her heart leap like a fish.

She crept carefully round Richard's sugar tree. Just in case any pagan ladies, in frocks flimsy as moths' wings, had got themselves stuck. "It was a bit unsporting of him – to trap them like that," she thought, frowning. There were no ladies there – she didn't expect it. It wasn't like pagans to fall for the same trick twice.

She saw swans like pale ghosts on the dark lake. Could it be them? They could shape-shift like witch doctors, if they wanted to.

With all her senses alert, she reached the pagan hill and rapped on it smartly with the frying-pan. She rattled the rusty padlock on the door.

"I know you're in there! Don't pretend you're not. I know you're listening." She had no time to be lady-like. She got straight to the point.

"I want you to do right by Bessie. You know her, don't you? She sits on this hill and croaks, 'Let me in. Let me in.' Well, you take her back into your kingdom. Give her what's owing to her – she's been waiting a beastly long time. Make her a princess and be nice to her." Alice thought that was worth repeating. "Do you hear what I say? Be *nice* to her."

Alice paused. The pagans stayed silent. There was no knowing what they were thinking. Alice would almost have welcomed their anger. She'd expected them to be angry – outraged at her cheek. To come screaming through the trees at her, fierce as cats, casting mischievous spells. She clutched Cook's frying-pan to her chest. She thought, "I hope this protects me against pagan magic." But nothing star-tling happened; not even a rustling in the leaves.

Her voice, when she spoke again, sounded reedy and frail. But she was determined to have her say. Bessie's future happiness depended on it.

"If you don't take Bessie in, then I'm going to give her this photo." Alice whisked the photo out of her coat like a conjurer and held it up. "Look what a good picture it is," she said. "That's taken using an Ilford Chromatic plate. It's sharp as sharp, isn't it?"

She stashed the photo safely away again. Then carried on in a rush of words: "You're still a secret now. No one is interested in you, except me and Bessie, but you know what Bessie is like – such a prattler. If I give it to her she'll show it to everyone and you'll be pestered to death – there'll be a thousand photographers and reporters and such in these woods and you'll be driven out of your ancient kingdom. So I'd take in Bessie if I were you and, if you do, I'll come here and rip this photo into little pieces, I promise, you'll be able to see me doing it. . ."

Alice stopped, breathless. "That's told 'em," she thought. Had she said enough? There was one other thing she longed to ask: "Oh and by the way, if it's not too much trouble, could you take my scars away? Make my skin smooth again like the princess in the photo? Please? Please?"

But she dared not say it. She didn't want to push them too far. Besides, it sounded too much like begging. And begging never works with pagans.

She gave a shaky smile – and wondered if anyone else, in the whole history of England, had ever tried to blackmail a pagan.

"But I'm not from here," she thought. "I'm that freakish child from Africa. And I do things as *I* choose."

She'd done a desperately reckless thing. She couldn't be sure it had worked. But she felt wonderfully

90

light-headed and exhilarated as she walked back to the Big House, with Cook's frying-pan dangling from her hand. Even her back didn't itch any more. She thought, happily, "I told those pagans. Didn't I just?"

She just hoped they believed her. Because, whatever happened, she didn't intend to give Bessie the photo. She didn't want those pagans driven away, any more than Bessie did. Or these woods to lose their magic. It was strange – there were mysteries here and things to be scared of. But she felt more alive now than at any number of tea parties, fretting about whether her gloves should be off or on.

The woods were all silver and grey in the moonlight. She glanced over her shoulder once or twice. But no pagans pursued her. They were probably too busy debating what to do. She imagined those pagans breaking off from their dancing and wild merry-making, sitting round a council table, with serious faces.

"I'm sure they'll agree to take Bessie in," Alice reassured herself." It would be such a *little* thing to do. And wouldn't she just *love* it down there. She'd be in clover!"

Alice grinned, suddenly. She was thinking of Princess Bessie, swishing round in golden frocks, stamping her tiny foot and lording it over all those servants. "Bring me bread and treacle! Polish my jelly moulds until they sparkle!"

"She'll be blissfully happy… But I'm going to miss that Bessie, when she goes back to the pagan kingdom," thought Alice, feeling hot tears stinging her eyelids. Although it perked her up no end to think that Richard would still be here.

She was just thinking, "I could become quite interested in taking pictures; I wonder if Aunt will lend me her Kodak," when she realized she'd missed the path. She was in an unknown part of the wood. Lost among great bushy rhododendrons.

She turned round, bewildered, and walked slap-bang into the pagan lady. The same one Richard had snapped for his photo. The lady glowed milky-white in the moonlight. She looked just as she did in his picture – windswept hair, her arms flung up, as if she was trying to flee. But this lady couldn't flee from anything. She was fixed to a plinth. She was a statue, made out of stone.

CHAPTER EIGHT

Alice stretched out a shaky hand. She thought she might be mistaken – that the pagan lady might be warm and alive. Might vanish, *puff*, in a swirl of stars when she was touched. Or even shape-shift into a bird and fly away.

But the pagan lady stayed right where she was, frozen into that stance. She was solid stone and cold as death. She wasn't going to change into anything. A slug slithered up her arm and left a slimy trail. A spider was busy building webs between her fingers.

She wasn't even tiny. She was human size, the same as Alice.

Alice frowned. Her head was buzzing with explanations. Had a cruel spell been cast on the princess – since this morning when her photo was taken – to turn her into stone? You never knew with pagans. They looked like fine lords and ladies but, sometimes, they could be as spiteful as children—

"So you've found her then," said a quiet voice behind her.

Alice spun round. It was Richard, with his camera slung over his shoulder and a bag of photography gear. He was out sugaring trees for moths. He put the bag down. "See here, I feel pretty guilty about all this," he told her. "I should have said something straightaway—"

"Said what?" demanded Alice.

"Look, I thought you knew all along," Richard struggled on. "I never dreamed you *believed* in all this pagan stuff, same as Bessie. I thought it was a bit of a wheeze—"

"A *wheeze*?" repeated Alice, completely baffled.

"I thought you were playing a *joke* on Bessie," said Richard defensively. "Anyone who believes in pagans deserves to have their leg pulled now and again."

"Are you trying to tell me," said Alice, looking from him to the statue, back to him again, "that pagans don't really exist?"

"COURSE THEY DON'T!" thundered Richard, relieved that she'd caught on at last. "Nobody round here believes in 'em. Except Bessie, of course."

Alice's mind was rebelling – her thoughts twittering everywhere like bats in a cave.

"But they take jelly moulds and kettles from the Big House kitchen," she spluttered. "Where do jelly moulds go if *they* don't take 'em?"

It was Richard's turn to be mystified: "Eh?"

"Bessie swore blind they took them. And the photo – what about your photo?"

She dragged the photo out of her pocket and waved it in his face, as evidence. Showers of salt came out with it. Richard stared but all he said was: "I'm glad you didn't give that photo to Bessie."

He'd also noticed she'd got her coat on inside-out and she was carrying a small frying-pan. He didn't comment on that either. She was from Africa after all and, by all accounts, they had some very strange customs in Africa.

"Photos can't lie," pleaded Alice. Even to herself she sounded desperate.

"This one does," Richard told her, his voice an odd mixture of pride and apology. "It's a fake. *I* faked it. I exposed the same glass plate twice. I mean to say, I took two photos on it, first the cedar tree, then the statue. It was quite tricky, actually – I had to use the telephoto to make the statue look smaller – but I thought you *knew* I was going to fake it. I thought that's what you were *asking* me to do. I never dreamed ... I never dreamed –" He shrugged helplessly.

"But the pagan hill?" implored Alice. Her mind just wouldn't accept what he was saying. It refused to. "The underground kingdom?"

Richard had been ready to mock her for being such an innocent. Believing in pagans? You had to be a noodle-brain, like Bessie, to do that. But he could see that she was very upset. And he liked her because she wasn't a snob even though, living at the Big House, you'd expect her to be. Besides, you had to make allowances for someone who'd lived all their life in Africa.

"It's not a pagan hill," he explained patiently. "It's the old ice house. There's a key to it somewhere – I think Cook's probably got it. Anyhow, when the lake froze over, they used to chop the ice off and put it in there and use it for, oh, I don't know, to make iced puddings and such."

Alice could believe that bit. It rang true. Puddings were important in England. Very important.

"But there's nothing in there now," added Richard.

No palaces. No crystal castles. Alice saw them whisked away, like a genie back into its bottle.

"Look," said Richard. "I'm sorry if this is rather bad news."

Alice sighed. Then she said a strange thing. "Well – they either exist. Or they don't."

"They *don't*," Richard assured her.

"That's a great pity," murmured Alice, still shell-shocked. She was trying hard to come to terms with it. But there seemed to be a great empty hole in her mind, where those pagans had been.

No pagan princesses. No fine clothes or beautiful body for Bessie.

"Oh no," thought Alice, who'd just realized the grim implications. "It's a black look-out for Bessie! She isn't a changeling, nor a pagan princess. She's just the gamekeeper's daughter."

She was just Bessie. That's all she was. With no hope of ever being anything different.

Richard couldn't stop talking about how he faked the photo. "I had to clean her up a bit," he said, jerking his thumb at the statue. "She was covered with moss. But she's perfect, isn't she? I mean to say, she *looks* like a pagan princess. She isn't though – she's Greek, I think. A nymph, my dad says. Probably being chased by a satyr, Dad says. They were always chasing nymphs, apparently—"

"But what are we going to tell Bessie?" Alice interrupted him, desperately. "Believing in pagans is her whole life!"

Richard couldn't see the problem. What did it matter if Bessie carried on thinking she was a changeling? It was stupid. But it seemed pretty harmless. He shrugged. "Don't tell her?" he suggested. Then he thought again and added. "But I shouldn't give her the photo if I were you. Perhaps you had better . . . just tear it up."

It hurt him to say that. Technically, it was the best photograph he'd ever taken. But he'd only thought of the challenge, not the consequences. Now he wished he'd never taken it. Alarm bells had rung in his brain this afternoon, as he'd realized, to his horror, that Alice believed in pagans too. He'd deliberately destroyed the negative. Let it smash to bits on the floor. He'd known right away that it would get him into a row. Deceiving Bessie was one thing – she was only Bessie, she didn't matter. But he'd never meant to deceive Alice.

"I think it's for the best," he said. Then he thought of something else. "Actually," he said. "I forgot. I saw Bessie just now –"

"Where was she?"

"Oh, just wandering about – you know, the way she does. She looked very down. And she was muttering away to herself. I didn't take much notice. Something about helping William – about being William's little helper? Who's William, anyhow?"

Alice's hands flew to her face in horror. Her mind was springing like a gazelle from one grotesque thought to another. "She wouldn't," she gasped out loud. "She wouldn't – would she?"

"Wouldn't what?" asked Richard.

But Alice was too wrapped up in her own night-mare thoughts.

She was thinking. "I *should* have given her the photo. What if she's in despair because she thinks there's no photo? And she doesn't want William wasting his life fretting and waiting and waiting – without even one sight of a pagan?"

Alice knew all about the fierce longings that blazed inside Bessie's frail body. She knew how vivid and powerful her imagination was. No one else under-stood that. Not even Aunt Evaline and Richard, who pitied her, but didn't have a clue what was going on in her head.

So Alice couldn't tell Richard what she feared. That Bessie might put William on the fire and believe she was doing him a great big favour. Believe he'd be whisked up the chimney without even his clothes getting scorched and taken back to his pagan home.

And it wasn't just Alice's fears that were making her tremble. She didn't have to imagine – she *knew* what it felt like, falling into flames.

She started running wildly. Then remembered that she was lost. "Which way to the path. Which way?"

"That way," said Richard. "But, I say, where are you off to?"

Alice turned round, her face screwed up with urgent anxiety. "To find Bessie. To tell her, 'Bessie, there are NO PAGANS. There are NO CHANGE-LINGS.' And then make her believe it."

She was off again. But she shouted back over her shoulder. "It's a matter of life and death."

Richard looked up at the statue. He appealed to it: "Do *you* know what the devil is going on?" But the statue just stared ahead, with blank, unseeing eyes.

CHAPTER NINE

Richard had been aiming to photograph hawk moths tonight. But he gave up his tree-sugaring plans.

"Oh, rot," he thought, sighing. "I suppose I'd better find Bessie. If it's a matter of life or death." He didn't really believe that – he thought Alice must be exaggerating.

"But there is obviously *something* wrong," he thought, uneasily. He was so worried that he abandoned his photography gear, stashed it under a rhododendron bush, so he could move faster. Usually, Richard and his camera were never parted.

Alice had disappeared in the direction of the Big House. "I don't see why Bessie should be up there," thought Richard. "Not at this time of night." Unless she was working late, polishing jelly moulds.

"I'll go to her house," he decided.

He had no idea what he would do when he found Bessie. "Just stand there having a little chat?" he suggested to himself. "Tell her, 'Oh, by the way, Bessie, pagans don't exist'? She'll think I'm off my head," he grumbled. He'd never cared before what Bessie would think of him. It had never even entered his mind.

He set off for the gamekeeper's cottage.

The moon washed the big lawn with silver, made it nearly bright as day. Halfway across it, Alice chucked Cook's iron frying-pan away. It was too heavy, it slowed her down. And after all, she didn't need protecting from pagans any more.

The scullery door was still unlocked – the butler hadn't done his rounds yet. Alice let out a a gasp of relief. But before she went in she ripped off her coat and turned it the right way out. She didn't want anyone to delay her with awkward questions.

She crashed through the kitchen doors. Blood was whistling in her ears; her heart nearly bursting –

Cook was there. Alice skidded to a halt, wild-eyed, panting, She circled Cook warily. "You big fat white Mama. You cockroach," she chanted inside her head. *"Get out of my way..."*

"Thought you was in bed," sniffed Cook, waddling across the kitchen. "Where you been sneaking off to? And look at that mud on your face. Come here. That needs a good scrub."

Cook turned round to get her scratchiest cloth. Alice shot off, up the narrow stone back stairs, heading for the front of the house.

"That child," said Cook, with a grim shake of her head. "Why did Master and Mistress ever take her on? No good'll come of it. They should have left her to stew in Africa."

Richard had just passed the gamekeeper's gibbet. He didn't give its grisly load a second glance. He'd already photographed it, last week, with an Ilford Chromatic plate.

Now he was peering through the windows of the gamekeeper's cottage. He'd seen red firelight glowing and two dark figures humped in chairs. Bessie didn't seem to be with them.

He crept round the back. He didn't intend to knock on the door, not unless he had to. He didn't like the gamekeeper. Bessie's dad was a weaselly little man, silent and surly. And he'd never heard her ma speak at all. Besides, how could he tell them. "I'm here to see Bessie"? That would be too humiliating.

He found Bessie's bedroom. At least, he guessed it was hers. Bessie had no brothers or sisters; they had died as babies. Richard knew that because his own dad, the doctor, had fought hard to save them.

He saw a small truckle bed. Its pillow made a dim, white square in the dark. But Bessie's head wasn't on the pillow. Her bedroom, only as big as a cupboard, was empty. There seemed to be nothing else in it but an old cane chair.

Then his eye caught a glint of gold. He pressed his nose closer to the window.

"A jelly mould," he breathed. "What's that doing in Bessie's bedroom?" In fact, there was a whole stack of them, all different sizes. And a kettle.

Richard raked around in his memory. He recalled Alice saying something about jelly moulds and kettles. About how pagans had borrowed them from the Big House kitchen. Bessie swore blind that they did.

"Bessie had them all the time," marvelled Richard. "She's got quite a collection there..."

He began to think there were depths to Bessie he'd never suspected.

It was a total surprise to him. Puzzling away at this new knowledge, he plodded back to the Big House, to tell Alice.

Alice had taken an age to get up to the nursery. It wasn't as late as she'd thought. There were still servants lurking about. One was closing the shutters in the ballroom. She darted past, quick as a gecko, and hid in an alcove behind a giant Ming vase. She didn't want to be challenged – she was supposed to be safely tucked up in bed.

She set off again, keeping a sharp look-out.

Strangely, her heart was only fluttering now. She'd even begun to think, like Richard, that she'd got carried away. Seeing the servants, doing all their normal, everyday duties, had put a brake on her runaway brain.

"Bessie *wouldn't*. . ." she'd almost convinced herself.

Then she pushed open the nursery door. It was a swing door, soundproofed with thick layers of green baize. And saw Bessie, all alone, in a rocking chair by a blazing fire – with William in her arms.

Bessie didn't see her. She was too busy crooning to the baby, some tender little song. She wrapped his shawl tightly round him and kissed him. To Alice's horrified gaze, it seemed like a last farewell. Then she got up from the chair—

"No!" screamed Alice frantically. She clamped her hands over her own ears, she didn't know why.

Her brain ordered her, *"Don't yell. Don't startle Bessie – she might do something stupid."*

"Bessie. Listen," Alice started again, trying to keep her voice gentle. She held out a calming hand. "Bessie – there are NO pagans –"

Down in the kitchen, Cook was treating herself to a small tipple of sweet sherry, when Richard walked in. "Master Richard!" she said surprised. "Is the doctor here then? And where's that camera of yours?"

"I'm not taking pictures," explained Richard quickly. "I'm looking for Alice."

"It's a quarter to nine," Cook disapproved. But the sherry had made her mellow. And besides, she had washed her hands of Alice. "What that child does is her own business. *I'm* not responsible," she'd decided.

"I believe she's upstairs," she told Richard, easing her bottom more comfortably into the chair.

"Can I go up then?" asked Richard.

Cook tossed her head, as if to say, "Do what you like. I don't want no part of it." So Richard crossed the grey flagstones.

He was just opening the door to the back stairs when he had a sudden, rogue thought.

"Cook," he asked her, with his most charming smile. "Do you happen to know where the key is. To that old ice house by the lake?"

"What do you want with that?" said Cook.

"I don't *want* it," said Richard. "I just wondered where it was, that's all."

Cook looked suspicious. But she couldn't immediately think of a reason for not answering.

"Bessie's got it," she told Richard. "She found it one day in a drawer and took a fancy to it. Tried to steal it, the little thief – copped her red-handed. And I'm just giving her a piece of my mind when Mistress comes in. And Mistress says she can have it! Not that it's any use to anyone. Bessie carries it round in her pocket – she won't be parted from it." Cook took another sip of sherry. "Who knows what's going on in that girl's head?"

Richard was wondering that too. He thought of Bessie, pounding away at the pagan hill, even kicking it with her boots. Crying, "Let me in, let me in," when she had the key to the door all the time.

"Why didn't she let *herself* in?" Richard asked himself. He couldn't make any sense of it. He had a lot to tell Alice, when he found her upstairs.

106

*   *   *

The fire in the nursery grate seemed to fill the room. It crackled and spat. The thought of William, dumped in those flames, gripped Alice's mind and she instantly felt the old panic – that hot, sick, dizzy feeling; those sweating hands. With a superhuman effort, she forced herself to ignore it. She tore her eyes away from the fire and fixed all her attention on Bessie.

"Give me the baby, Bessie," she coaxed.

Bessie stood by the fire, cradling William. She didn't show any signs of giving the baby up. She just stared at Alice, with her mouth hanging slightly open.

Alice measured the distance between her and Bessie, wondering if she could pounce and snatch the baby from her. She moved slowly forward, talking all the time –

"He isn't a changeling Bessie. Don't put him in the fire. He won't go up the chimney – he'll get burned, Bessie. It'll be terrible."

Bessie seemed more witless than ever. Still, she wouldn't hand over the baby. Instead she backed off two more steps. She held him tighter and stared, dumbstruck, as her friend crept, cat-like, towards her.

Alice couldn't think what to do to get through to Bessie. Then suddenly, she knew. She struggled out of her coat. Bessie only stared, her eyes popping. Alice reached over her shoulder and tore open the top buttons of her dress.

The baby woke up. He started that thin wailing noise.

"Shhh, shhh," crooned Bessie, automatically rocking him. But she didn't take her eyes off Alice.

Feverishly, Alice turned her back, pulled her long hair to one side. She had on corsets and petticoats but you could see enough. You could see thick, shiny scars snaking along her shoulders.

"Look," she demanded. She was shaking but determined. "Look, Bessie. My whole back's like that. I was burned in a fire when I was little. I can't describe the pain – it's awful. I screamed and screamed, I'll never forget it. And I'll have these scars the rest of my life."

She let her hair drop like a veil so it hid her back. Then turned again to face Bessie. Had it worked? Had she shocked Bessie into giving up William? She couldn't believe it – the fire spat a shower of red sparks but Bessie still clutched that baby, as if she would never let him go. Except that she moved, one step towards the fire.

Alice heard her own voice getting shriller. "Did you see my back? Say something, Bessie," she begged. "Do you understand? There are no pagans, Bessie. No pagans."

"She already knows that."

Alice leapt round. Richard had come in. He was standing, very quietly, by the nursery doors. "How long has he been there? Did he see my back?" Agonized questions raced through Alice's brain. Then she realized what Richard had just said. Bessie too, seemed to be coming back to life.

"Wait a minute," protested Bessie. She sounded outraged but to Alice's intense relief she moved away from the fire. She stalked across the room and put William down in his crib.

She turned back to confront them. "Wait a minute!" Bessie boomed again, shaking a twiggy finger at them. "You didn't think I would hurt that baby, did you? I was looking after him for Nurse. She said I was allowed. You ask her—"

"Shhh!" warned Richard. "Someone will hear."

Alice looked from Richard to Bessie, to the baby safe in his cot. She was floundering, completely out of her depth. She didn't have a clue what was going on. But one question kept tormenting her: "Did he see my back? Did he?"

"*Calm down, he couldn't have done,*" she soothed herself. Richard didn't seem repelled or disgusted. Instead he was asking Bessie something in a low, urgent voice.

"Show Alice what you keep in your pocket, Bessie. What you carry around with you, always."

Bessie looked mystified for a moment. Then she said, "Oh, you mean my key?"

William was gurgling, squirming about in his crib. Alice sneaked closer to him, just in case Bessie should change her mind and try snatching him up again. But Bessie didn't seem interested in the baby any more.

Instead, she was searching for something in her apron pocket. She pulled out a big key.

"It's the key to the old ice house," Richard explained to Alice. "Bessie had it all the time."

"Course I had it," said Bessie, scowling. "That's no secret, is it?"

"And when I looked into her bedroom just now, there was a kettle and lots of jelly moulds. The pagans didn't take 'em, did they Bessie? You took 'em, and said the pagans did it."

Bessie hung her head, shuffling her feet and sulking. Eventually, she mumbled something.

"What?" demanded Alice. "What did you say?"

"I was only borrowing them – I would've put them back."

Alice stared, astonished, at her friend. She was still struggling to understand. Could it be true? That Bessie talked about pagans as if she really believed – yet all the time she *knew* they didn't exist?

"I can't believe it. You knew all along you weren't a changeling? But you told everyone you were!" began Alice, furiously.

"There's no law against it, is there?" said Bessie, sticking out her pointy chin, defiantly.

"You *knew* there weren't any pagans?"

"Yes," said Bessie bluntly, in the same unapologetic voice.

"You could have told me," said Alice. Angry tears blurred her eyes. She dashed them away with the sleeve of her dress. "You could have told *me*."

"What you crying for?" said Bessie, frowning up into Alice's face, genuinely concerned.

Alice sprang at her. "You, you—!" And was about to grab her when the nursery door opened and Aunt Evaline sailed in, bringing great wafts of lavender perfume with her.

Alice stopped dead. Her whole body was trembling. She took deep, shuddering breaths to calm herself down. She dared not look Aunt Evaline in the face. She kept her eyes on the carpet.

But Aunt Evaline didn't notice anything was wrong.

"Oh, how sweet," she said. "The four of you together! What a cosy scene. Have you come to see William, Richard? Bessie has been so good with him, haven't you Bessie?" She patted Bessie on the head as if she was a good dog. Bessie glowed. "I think I shall take you off polishing jelly moulds," smiled Aunt Evaline, "and let you be Nurse's little helper."

She plucked William out of his crib, "Come on, my little man," and swept out of the room. She poked her head back in for a moment. "Oh, by the way, Alice. Your dress buttons seem to have popped. Get my maid to sew them back on tomorrow."

Cook would have approved – Alice's yellowy cheeks blushed as pink as English roses. She scrabbled at her back, trying to do up the buttons.

They waited, until Aunt Evaline was out of hearing. Neither Richard nor Bessie spoke.

Alice thought, "What do I feel like?"

She should have felt washed-out, so many emotions had shaken her body in the past few minutes. But instead she felt horribly used and betrayed. She didn't trust her new friends any more.

"I suppose you thought it was a frightfully good *wheeze*?" she accused them, bitterly. "Oh how jolly! There's someone coming from Africa, she must be stupid. We'll tell her some silly tale about pagans, make her believe it."

Bessie looked at her as if she'd gone mad. Richard faltered, "I – I don't think it was like that."

But she was too distraught to listen. She had another suspicion. "Are you *sure* you don't believe in 'em?" she challenged Bessie. "I want to know that you don't. I want to know you're not going to hurt William."

"I wouldn't *never* do that. How can you think such a thing? I like babies! I'm really good with babies—"

"Open the pagan mound then," said Alice, her head suddenly clearing. "Then I'll know you don't really believe." She flung on her coat and dragged Bessie across the room by the wrist.

"Get off! Get off!" wailed Bessie. "I thought you was nice. You're beastly really. Why don't you go back to Africa and stay there?"

But Alice didn't slacken her grip. She was merciless. She pulled Bessie down the stairs with Richard

112

stumbling after. He said nothing. He thought it was safer – he didn't want Alice turning on him.

Alice hauled a protesting Bessie down the back stairs, across the moonlit lawn, all the way through the woods, past the stone lion and the sugar tree. She didn't stop until they reached the pagan hill. Then she let Bessie go. "Open it," she ordered her. "Go on, open it."

The pagan hill glowed at them. There had been some light rain. On every grass stem a water droplet quivered. They sparkled in the moonlight like diamonds.

"Ow," said Bessie, rubbing her wrist. "You hurt me! I never knew you was so cruel."

"Open it," said Alice, menacingly.

"All right," grumbled Bessie, hauling the big key out of her pocket. "But the lock is all rusty. It might not work."

Richard stood silently in the background, watching.

Bessie put the key in the lock and gave it the tiniest twist. "It just won't open," she said.

"Let me try," said Alice, prising Bessie's fingers off the key and wrenching it round in the lock. "See, it does work."

Bessie shrugged.

"I'm going to open the door now," warned Alice. The little door creaked and protested. She yanked it almost off its hinges. "It's open," she panted. Richard moved forwards, so he could see inside.

There was nothing down there. Just a dark, dank, slimy hole, brick-lined like a well.

"See, I told you it was just the old ice house," said Richard. "There's some interesting mosses down there. Pity they're too far down to photograph." He suddenly wondered if his camera was safe, all by itself under the rhododendron bush. "Half a sec," he said. "I just have to fetch something."

Bessie was staring down into the empty hole. So was Alice. There were no pagans. It was a certainty now. And Alice realized that she'd dragged Bessie here not to prove to Bessie that there were no pagans – but to prove it, once and for all, to herself.

She frowned. She would have to make it up to Bessie now, for being so rough with her. But just to make absolutely sure, she asked Bessie. "Look down there, Bessie. There's no pagan kingdom, is there?"

"I know," sighed Bessie.

"What do you see then?" persisted Alice. She thought Bessie might say, "Nothing. It's just a black hole."

But that familiar starry look came into Bessie's eyes. She squinted into the ice house and said, "Do you know, I think I can spy a crystal palace down there. Just the tops of its towers."

"For Heaven's sake," cried Alice, at her wits' end. "No you *don't*, Bessie. There's *nothing* down there."

"I see palaces where other folk see scummy ponds," insisted Bessie, with a look of stubborn pride on her face. "And gold coins where they see beans. And rich clothes where they see rags."

"*Bessie!*" warned Alice. She wanted to shake her. "Stop being a brat! Look here, you could have got into this hill, any time you liked. And you *know* pagans don't take jelly moulds, because *you* took 'em. You don't believe in pagans, do you, Bessie? You always *knew* you weren't really a changeling."

"Course I did," said Bessie, scornfully, as if it was obvious. "I'm not daft, you know. But I was *pretending*, wasn't I? I'm really good at pretending. There's no law against it, is there? Everyone's got to have dreams."

CHAPTER TEN

"That Bessie," said Richard next day. "She's a deep one, isn't she?"

Alice's back felt sore again. It was itching like mad. She wriggled her shoulders to try and make it stop. Her one consolation was that Richard hadn't seen it. If he had, he wouldn't be sitting talking to her now, beneath the sugar tree, as friendly as before.

Alice nodded. "Bessie's deep as the ocean." She and Bessie had made friends again. You couldn't stay angry with Bessie for long. "I'll put the jelly moulds back," Bessie had said. "Honest I will. And the kettle."

Alice didn't know whether to be glad or sorry that she'd been mixed up in Bessie's pretending games. For a while, she'd believed in those pagans absolutely. They had been living, breathing beings. She still found it difficult to shake them off.

Through the trees, she could see a swan on the lake. And she thought, before she could stop herself, "Is that one of them?"

Bessie suddenly appeared and flung herself down beside them. "Is that one of them?" asked Bessie, pointing to the swan.

"Bessie, stop it!" said Alice, angrily.

Bessie sulked and stuck out her lower lip like a fat, pink slug. "I'm only pretending," she said. "Don't tell me off."

Alice relented. "So long as you know they don't *really* exist."

"But I always knew that," Bessie pointed out, smugly.

"Bessie," said Alice. "You're a very strange person."

"I know," said Bessie cheerfully, leaping up.

"Where are you going?"

"I got no time to chat, I'm in an awful hurry," said Bessie, looking important. "I'm helping Nurse. Isn't it just dreamy? Those rotten old cows, Cook and Bertha, can't boss me around no more. I'm *upstairs* now. Only Nurse can tell me what to do. And she's nice."

And Bessie bustled off in the direction of the Big House.

Richard asked Alice, "Did you say you could borrow a Kodak?"

"Yes," said Alice. "Aunt Evaline says I can have it. As long as I take some pictures of William."

"Babies?" said Richard in disgust. "You'll need a short exposure for that. They never stop squirming about."

Just hearing that word, "squirming" was enough to set Alice off. She had to scratch her itchy back against the sugar tree, desperate to get some relief. She'd just realized, "Ugh, this tree's sticky," when Richard dropped his bombshell. "Are your scars hurting you today?" he asked her.

It set her world rocking again. Just when she thought that things were settling down. Her brain gibbered at her. "*He saw my back.*" But the words that came stuttering from her lips were. "What? What did you say?"

"I've seen much worse than that," boasted Richard, fiddling about screwing the lens on his camera. "My dad's a doctor, remember. He treats lots of burns. Yours have healed up beautifully, haven't they?"

Alice stared at him, in amazed disbelief. She'd never imagined the word "beautiful" applied to her scars. He even spoke as though she should be proud of them! She was caught completely off-guard. Her ideas about herself turned on their heads. And before she could stop herself, she'd told Richard about her accident.

"I got burned in a cooking fire in Africa. When I was little."

"Did you?" said Richard. "Bad luck... I say though, when you lived in Africa, did you ever see a leopard or a lion? Wouldn't I just love to photograph one of them..."

And that was the end of his interest in Alice's scars.

Instead, Miss Silent-and-Say-Nothing found herself telling him about the time she and Mayamiko had been stalked through the bush. She told him lots of things about Africa. She told him she felt homesick and missed her ma and pa dreadfully. He didn't say, "You ungrateful wretch!" He didn't think, like all the others, that a new life in England was all a poor missionary's daughter should ever want, or dream of.

He said, "I should miss that place dreadfully too. Did you say there are giant moths as big as dinner plates?"

She could see his eyes light up. Calculating how much sugar solution he'd need to catch one of those. He made himself a promise. "I'll go there one day," he said.

That afternoon, after Richard had gone back home, Alice set out to find her other friend, Bessie. Bessie wasn't on the top floor with Nurse and William. "She's gone home," said Nurse. "She was a very useful little helper all this morning. We're very pleased with her."

As Alice piled on her outdoor clothes, salt puffed out of her pocket. That made her think of Cook's frying-pan, abandoned on the lawn. It was hard to believe that only yesterday, she'd been out there blackmailing pagans. Threatening them, "Take Bessie in, *or else*..." And now she knew for a fact they didn't exist. It had been a very nasty shock. But she was getting used to it – especially now her mind was busy with other things.

A funny thing happened, though, when she passed the ballroom. As usual, she stared in, entranced by the dazzling mirrors. But this time, something made her step over the threshold. Her boots clattered on the glossy wood floor. She stood in front of a tall mirror, critically inspecting herself.

This time, her reflection didn't make her shy away like a frightened pony. "I've got shiny hair," she decided, peering closer. "And quite nice eyes." Then something else in the mirror caught her attention. It twirled past in the sunny room behind her. It was light as a dandelion seed. She had one confused glimpse of a white, wispy dress, of slim arms flung up, dancing. Then it was gone.

She spun round, her heart fluttering with expectation. Was it –? Of course not – there was nothing there.

"Huh," she chided herself, clattering out of the room. "You haven't *quite* got over these pagans yet, have you?"

In the woodland, she shuffled through bluebells, automatically patting the pug-faced lion as she passed. She might have gone for a quick look at that other statue – the one she still called "the pagan lady", even though she knew now it wasn't. But she couldn't remember exactly where it was.

Bessie was sitting perched on the pagan hill, drumming her heels and staring out over the lake at the swans. The pagan hill was locked again and Alice knew, without asking, that Bessie had the key in her apron pocket

Alice didn't call out to her straightaway. She stood watching her for a while. She wondered, rather sadly, what would happen to Bessie. How she would make her way in the world. But there was one thing Alice did know. It didn't make any difference that they'd unlocked the pagan hill, seen only a deep, dark hole inside. Bessie would go on, probably all her life, seeing castles where other folk saw deep, dark holes, gold coins where they saw beans, rich clothes where they saw rags.

"Why shouldn't she?" thought Alice. "There's no law against it, is there?"

And, at that moment, it didn't seem at all strange to her, or contradictory, that Bessie could believe, and *not* believe, at one and the same time.

Alice called out, "Hello, Bessie!"

Bessie swivelled round, her tiny goblin face made dreamy by all the wonderful visions she had inside her head.

Alice joined Bessie on the pagan hill and they both stared out at the swans. For a time, neither of them spoke.

Then Bessie asked, her eyes wide and innocent, "Are you and that Richard *sweethearts* then?"

"No!" said Alice hotly. But there was no denying she was tickled that Bessie thought so. "We are just doing photography together, that's all."

Bessie leapt off the pagan mound and dashed to the edge of the lake. From a safe distance, she called back. "Is that what you call it?" Then doubled up, in a fit of rude sniggering.

"I'll kill you when I get hold of you, Bessie!" yelled Alice, her sallow skin flushed bright pink with embarrassment. "No, I have a better idea. I'm going to turn you into a *cockroach*."

Bessie's teasing answer echoed over the water. "*Na, na, na, na, na.* You got to catch me first."

Bessie was getting away. But Alice stopped to do one thing. She reached into her coat pocket and took out Richard's photo. She held it up. And, in full view of the pagan mound, she ripped it slowly into little shreds and let the wind take it.

"There," she said – and it was hard to tell if she was talking to herself or someone else. "That's the end of that."

Then she went laughing after Bessie, through the trees.